FRANKLIN PARK PUBLIC LIBRARY
FRANKLIN PARK, ILL.

Each borrower is held responsible for all library material drawn on his card and for fines accruing on the same. No material will be issued until such fine has been paid.

All injuries to library material beyond reasonable wear and all losses shall be made good to the satisfaction of the Librarian.

Jimmy Gownley's AMELIA RULES!™

Speak Softee to Me

Atheneum Books for Young Readers
New York London Toronto Sydney

Spotlight

VISIT US AT
www.abdopublishing.com

Reinforced library bound edition published in 2011 by Spotlight, a division of the ABDO Group, 8000 West 78th Street, Edina, Minnesota 55439. Spotlight produces high-quality reinforced library bound editions for schools and libraries. Published by agreement with Atheneum Books for Young Readers, an imprint of Simon & Schuster Children's Publishing Division.

Antheneum Books for Young Readers
An imprint of Simon & Schuster Children's Publishing Division
1230 Avenue of the Americans, New York, NY 10020

Printed in the United States of America, Melrose Park, Illinois.
052010
092010
This book contains at least 10% recycled materials.

Library of Congress Cataloging-in-Publication Data

Gownley, Jimmy.
Amelia in Speak Softee to me / Jimmy Gownley. -- Reinforced library bound ed.
p. cm. -- (Jimmy Gownley's Amelia rules! ; #5)
Summary: When Amelia's divorced father invites her friends along on their father-daughter camping trip, she does not respond graciously.
ISBN 978-1-59961-791-6
1. Graphic novels. [1. Graphic novels. 2. Fathers and daughters--Fiction. 3. Divorce--Fiction. 4. Camping--Fiction.] I. Title. II. Title: Speak Softee to me.
PZ7.7.G69Ams 2010
741.5'973--dc22

2010006196

Spotlight

All Spotlight books have reinforced library bindings and are manufactured in the United States of America.

With Love and Thanks
to Mom and Dad...

With appreciation for
the Vision and Faith of
Joe, John, Jerry, and Bill...

And with gratitude for
the Patience and Friendship
of Michael...

This book is dedicated with love...
for Karen.

J-GN
AMELIA RULES
399-7163

Speak Softee
to Me

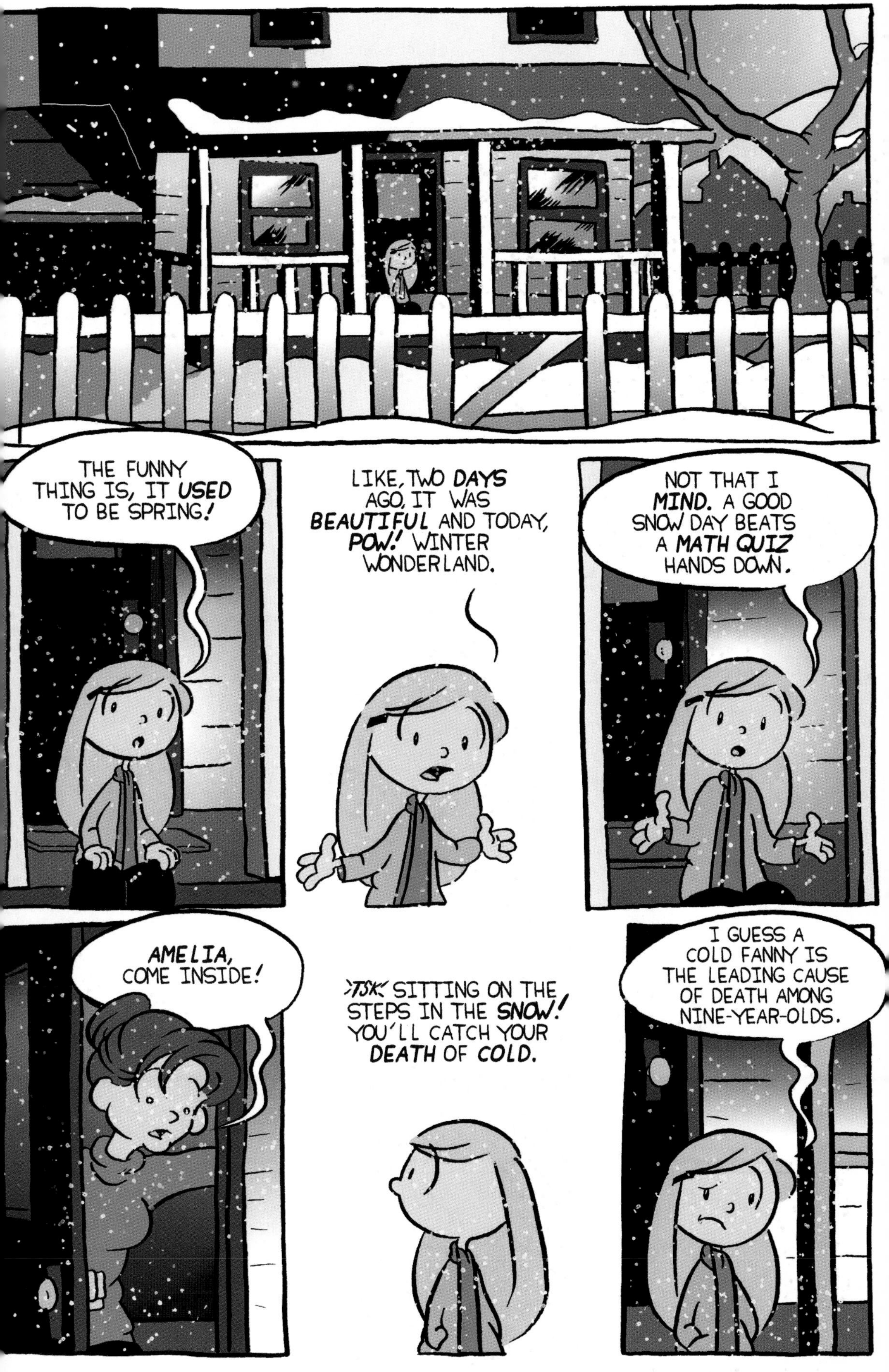
THE FUNNY THING IS, IT USED TO BE SPRING!
LIKE, TWO DAYS AGO, IT WAS BEAUTIFUL AND TODAY, POW! WINTER WONDERLAND.
NOT THAT I MIND. A GOOD SNOW DAY BEATS A MATH QUIZ HANDS DOWN.
AMELIA, COME INSIDE!
>TSK< SITTING ON THE STEPS IN THE SNOW! YOU'LL CATCH YOUR DEATH OF COLD.
I GUESS A COLD FANNY IS THE LEADING CAUSE OF DEATH AMONG NINE-YEAR-OLDS.

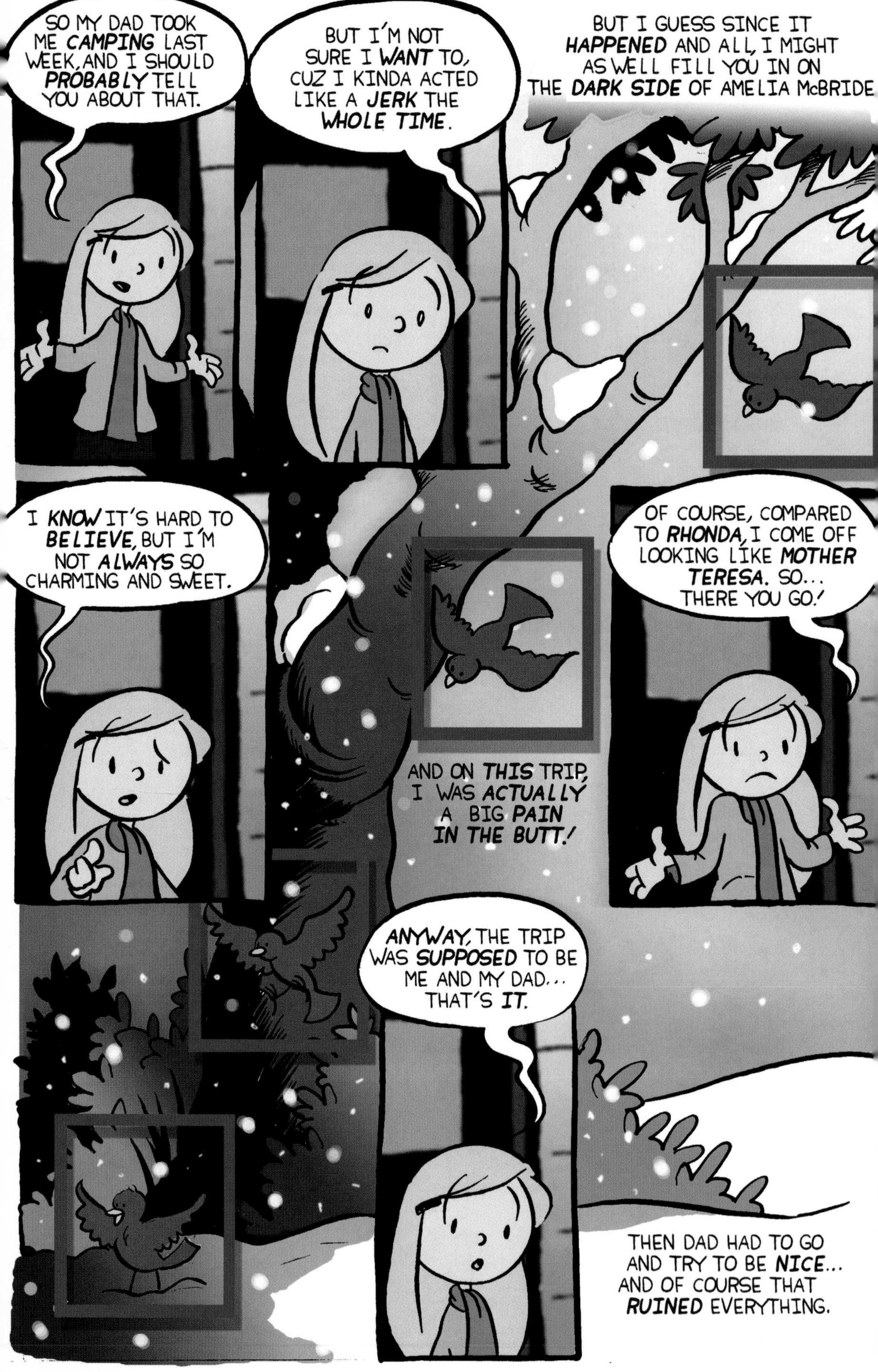

SO MY DAD TOOK ME CAMPING LAST WEEK, AND I SHOULD PROBABLY TELL YOU ABOUT THAT.
BUT I'M NOT SURE I WANT TO, CUZ I KINDA ACTED LIKE A JERK THE WHOLE TIME.
BUT I GUESS SINCE IT HAPPENED AND ALL, I MIGHT AS WELL FILL YOU IN ON THE DARK SIDE OF AMELIA McBRIDE.
I KNOW IT'S HARD TO BELIEVE, BUT I'M NOT ALWAYS SO CHARMING AND SWEET.
AND ON THIS TRIP, I WAS ACTUALLY A BIG PAIN IN THE BUTT!
OF COURSE, COMPARED TO RHONDA, I COME OFF LOOKING LIKE MOTHER TERESA. SO... THERE YOU GO!
ANYWAY, THE TRIP WAS SUPPOSED TO BE ME AND MY DAD... THAT'S IT.
THEN DAD HAD TO GO AND TRY TO BE NICE... AND OF COURSE THAT RUINED EVERYTHING.

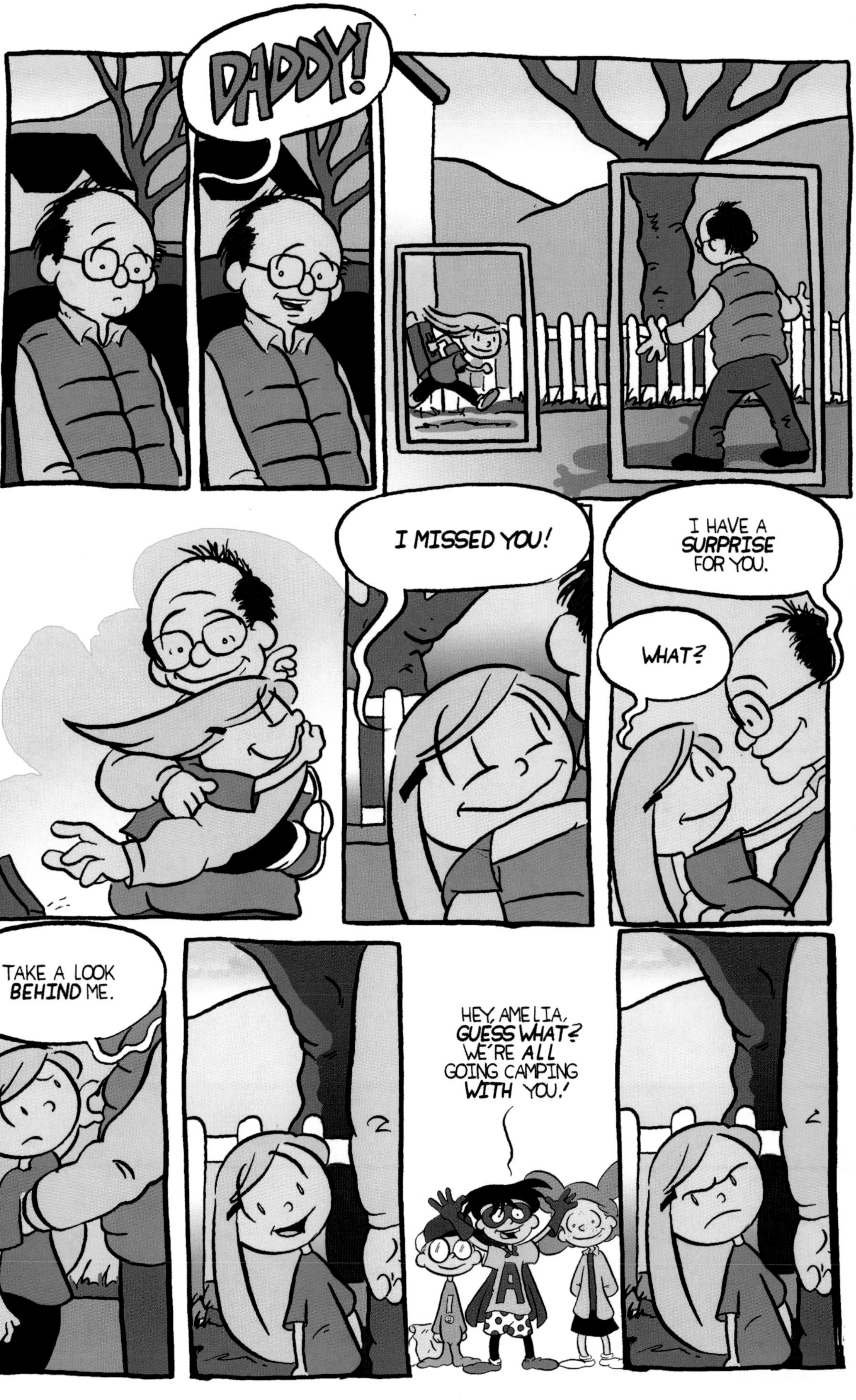
DADDY!
I MISSED YOU!
I HAVE A SURPRISE FOR YOU.
WHAT?
TAKE A LOOK BEHIND ME.
HEY, AMELIA, GUESS WHAT? WE'RE ALL GOING CAMPING WITH YOU!

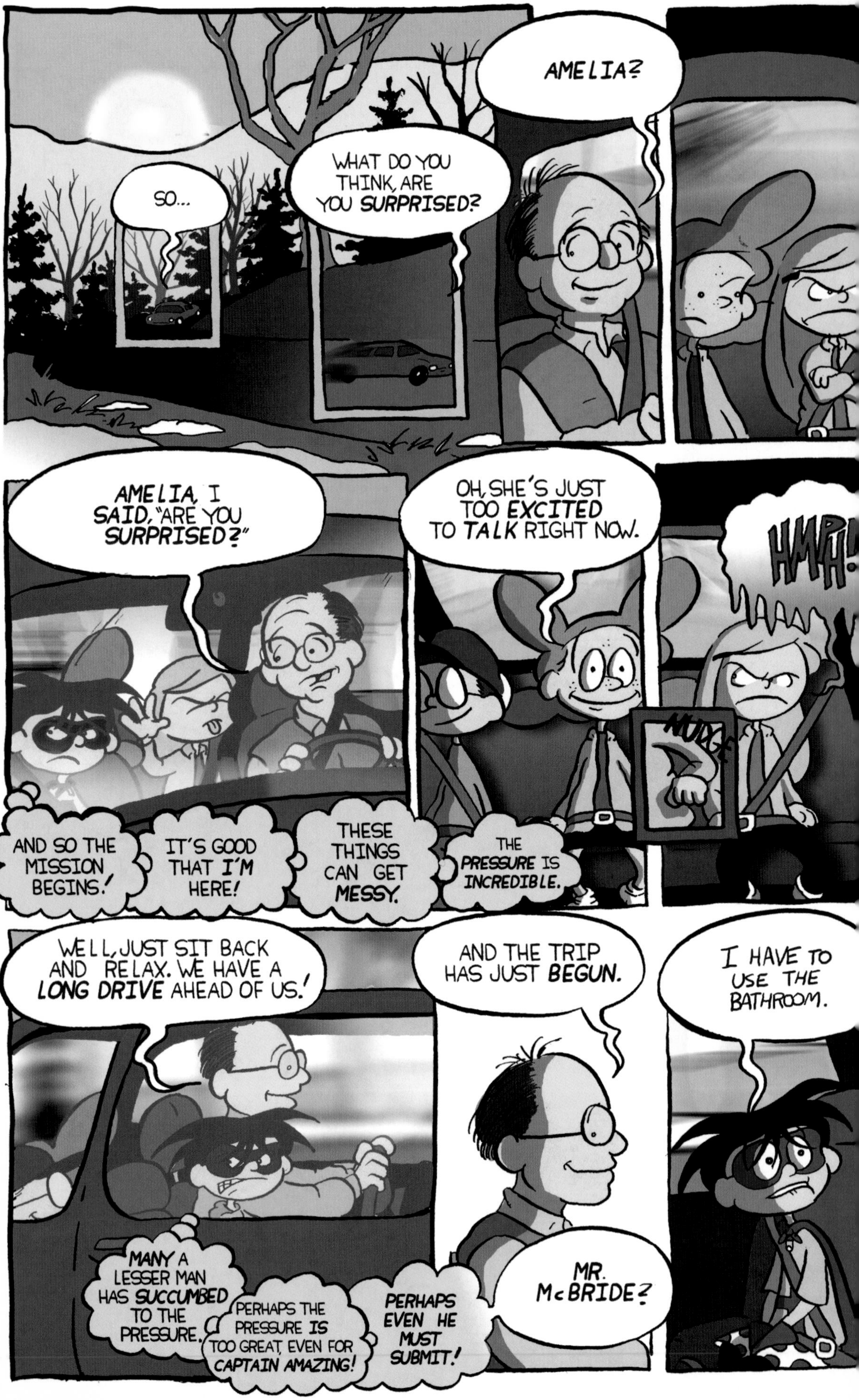
SO...
WHAT DO YOU THINK, ARE YOU SURPRISED?
AMELIA?
AMELIA, I SAID, "ARE YOU SURPRISED?"
AND SO THE MISSION BEGINS!
IT'S GOOD THAT I'M HERE!
THESE THINGS CAN GET MESSY.
OH, SHE'S JUST TOO EXCITED TO TALK RIGHT NOW.
THE PRESSURE IS INCREDIBLE.
NUDGE
HMPH!
WELL, JUST SIT BACK AND RELAX. WE HAVE A LONG DRIVE AHEAD OF US!
MANY A LESSER MAN HAS SUCCUMBED TO THE PRESSURE.
PERHAPS THE PRESSURE IS TOO GREAT, EVEN FOR CAPTAIN AMAZING!
PERHAPS EVEN HE MUST SUBMIT!
AND THE TRIP HAS JUST BEGUN.
MR. McBRIDE?
I HAVE TO USE THE BATHROOM.

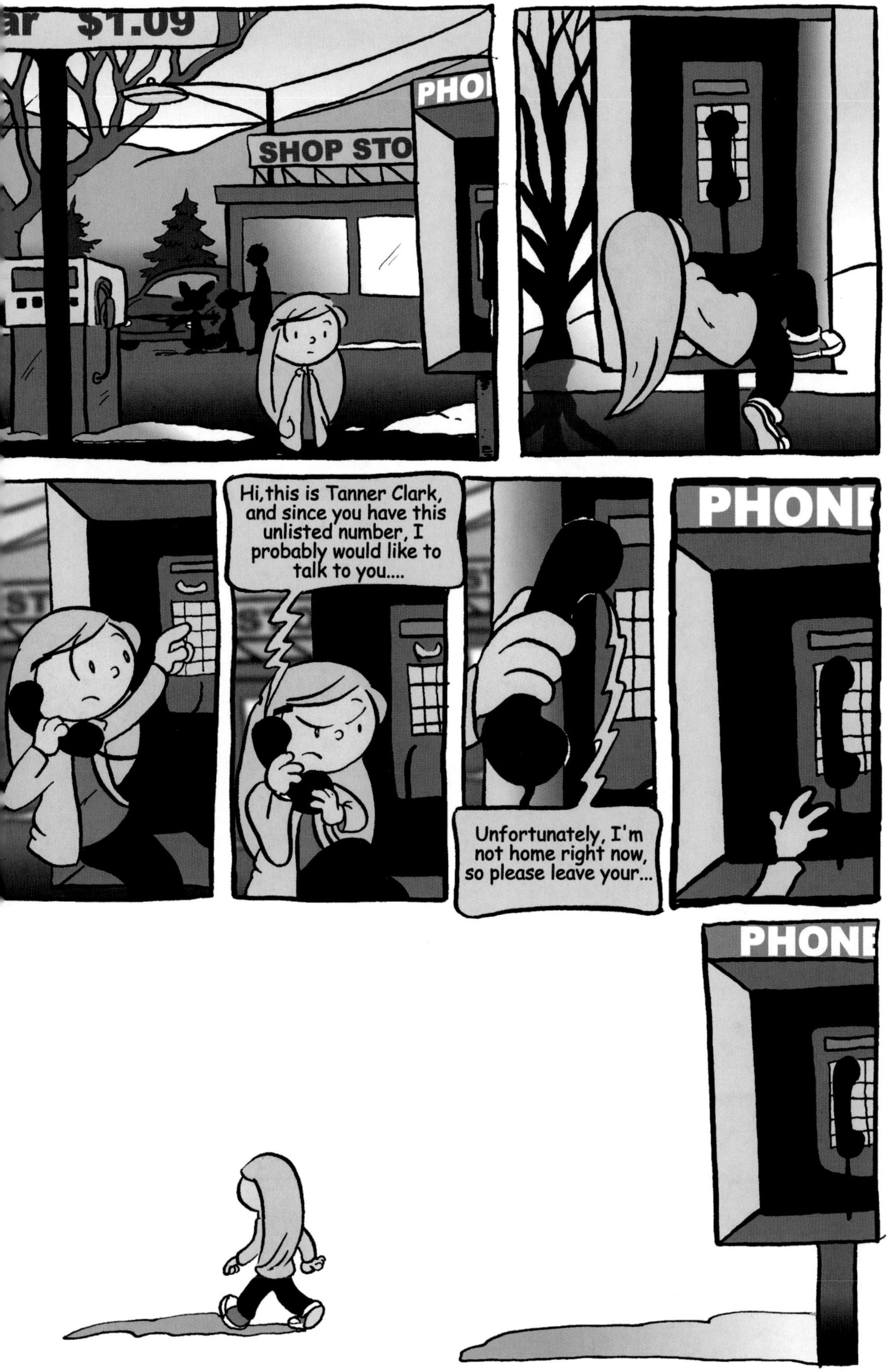

$1.09
PHO
SHOP STO
Hi, this is Tanner Clark, and since you have this unlisted number, I probably would like to talk to you....
Unfortunately, I'm not home right now, so please leave your...
PHONE
PHONE

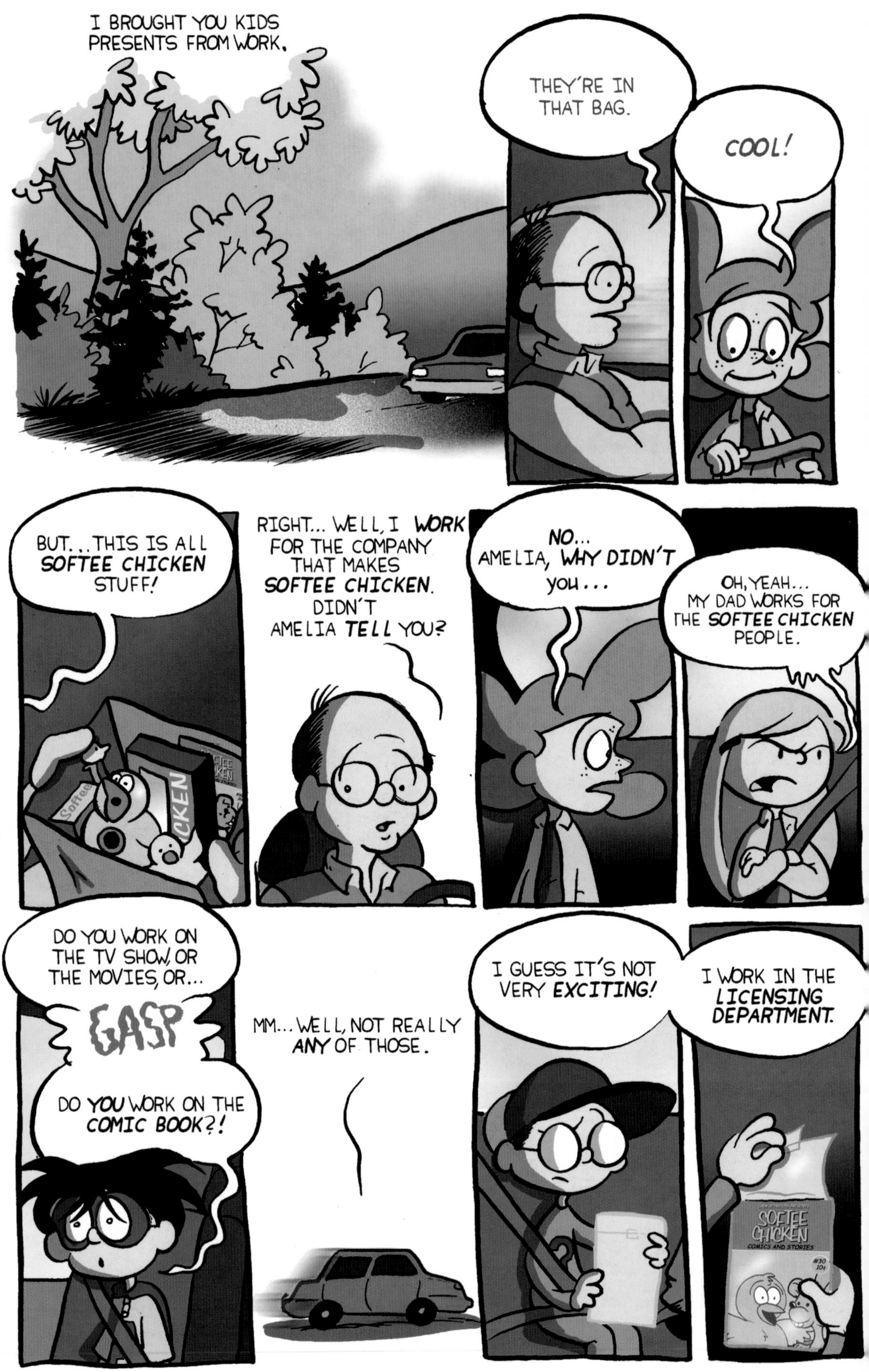
I BROUGHT YOU KIDS PRESENTS FROM WORK.
THEY'RE IN THAT BAG.
COOL!
BUT...THIS IS ALL SOFTEE CHICKEN STUFF!
RIGHT... WELL, I WORK FOR THE COMPANY THAT MAKES SOFTEE CHICKEN. DIDN'T AMELIA TELL YOU?
NO... AMELIA, WHY DIDN'T YOU...
OH, YEAH... MY DAD WORKS FOR THE SOFTEE CHICKEN PEOPLE.
DO YOU WORK ON THE TV SHOW, OR THE MOVIES, OR...
GASP
DO YOU WORK ON THE COMIC BOOK?!
MM... WELL, NOT REALLY ANY OF THOSE.
I GUESS IT'S NOT VERY EXCITING!
I WORK IN THE LICENSING DEPARTMENT.
SOFTEE CHICKEN
COMICS AND STORIES

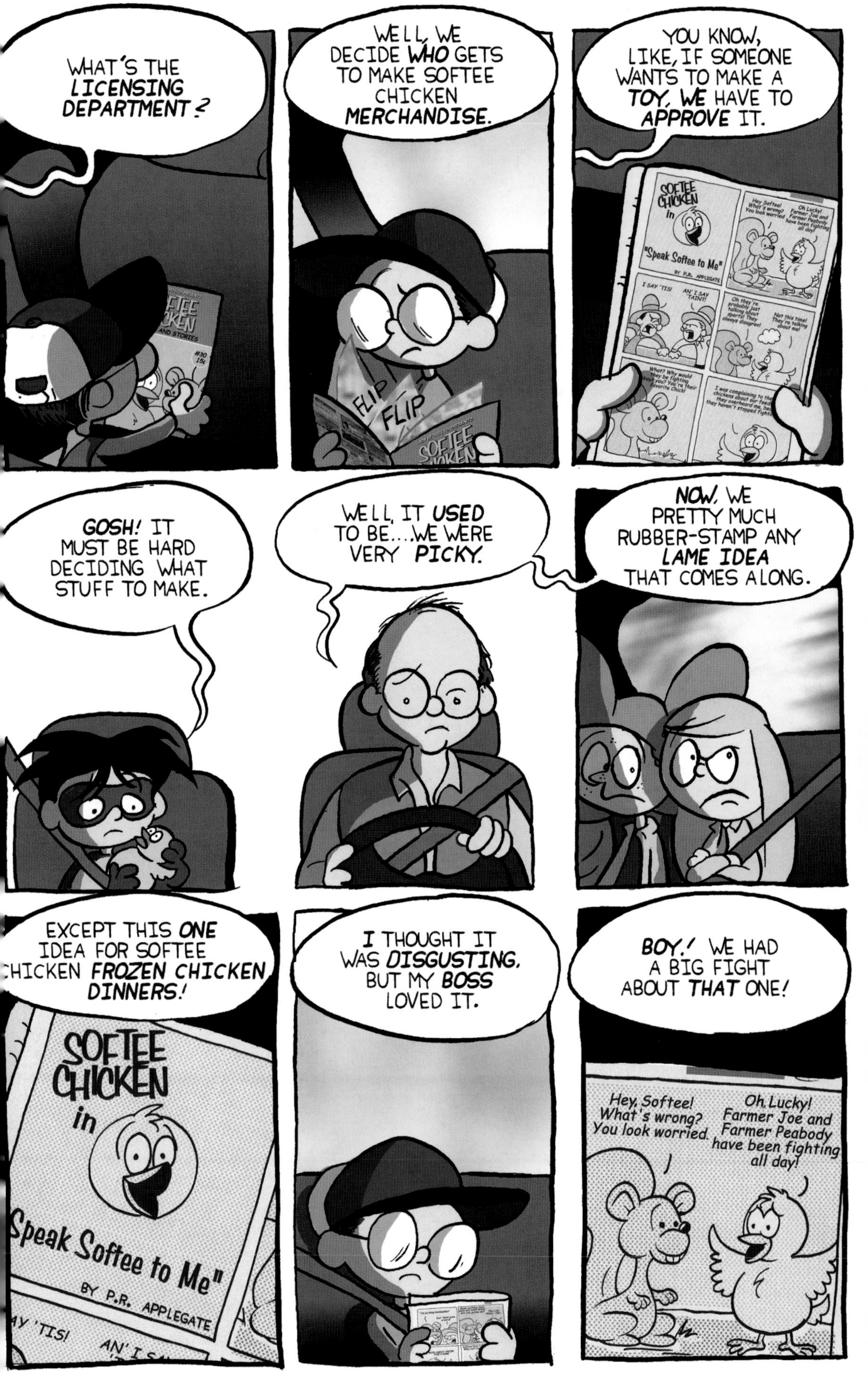
WHAT'S THE LICENSING DEPARTMENT?
WELL, WE DECIDE WHO GETS TO MAKE SOFTEE CHICKEN MERCHANDISE.
FLIP FLIP
YOU KNOW, LIKE, IF SOMEONE WANTS TO MAKE A TOY, WE HAVE TO APPROVE IT.
GOSH! IT MUST BE HARD DECIDING WHAT STUFF TO MAKE.
WELL, IT USED TO BE....WE WERE VERY PICKY.
NOW, WE PRETTY MUCH RUBBER-STAMP ANY LAME IDEA THAT COMES ALONG.
EXCEPT THIS ONE IDEA FOR SOFTEE CHICKEN FROZEN CHICKEN DINNERS!
SOFTEE CHICKEN in
"Speak Softee to Me"
BY P.R. APPLEGATE
I THOUGHT IT WAS DISGUSTING, BUT MY BOSS LOVED IT.
BOY! WE HAD A BIG FIGHT ABOUT THAT ONE!
Hey, Softee! What's wrong? You look worried.
Oh, Lucky! Farmer Joe and Farmer Peabody have been fighting all day!

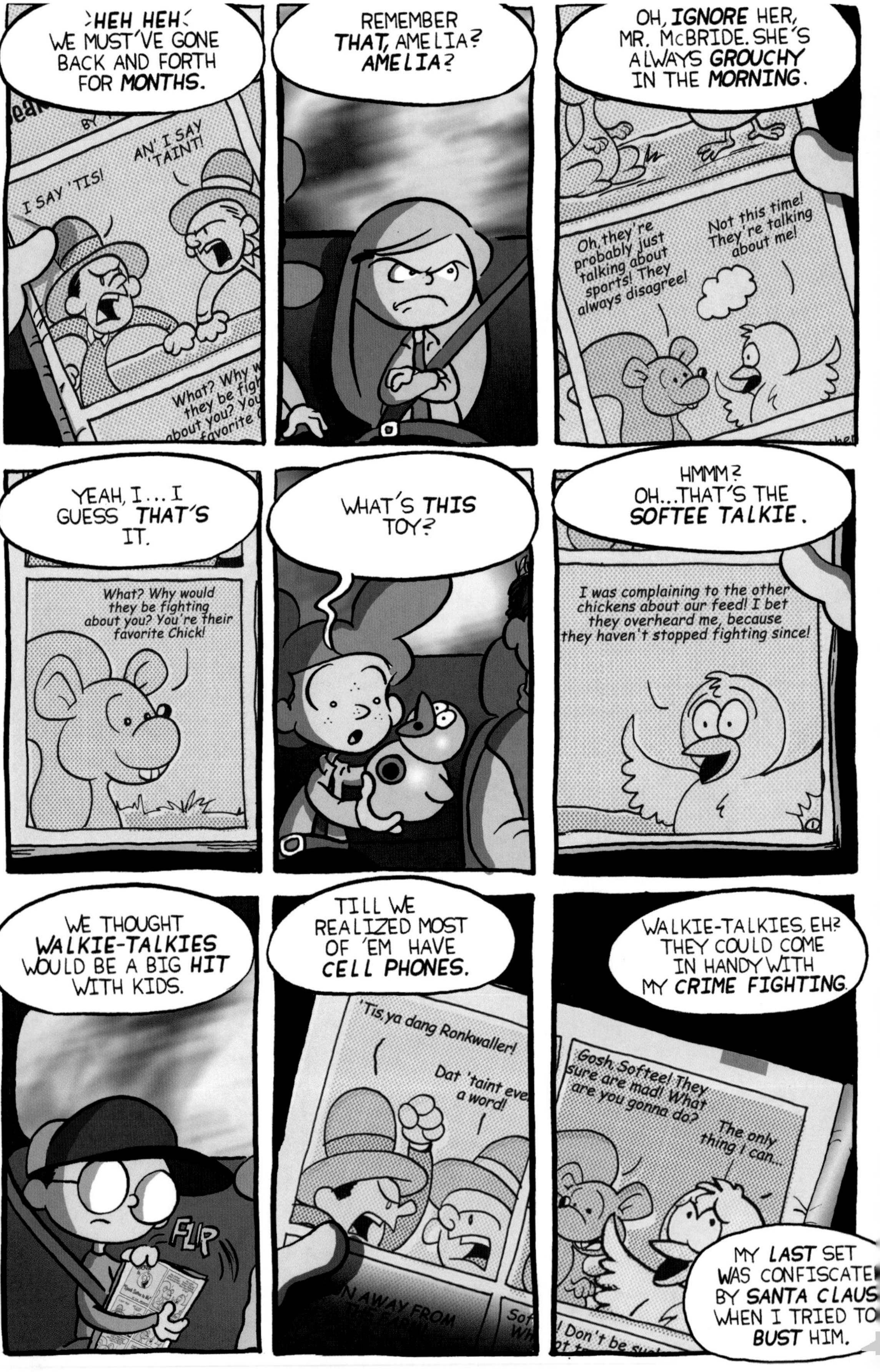

>HEH HEH<
WE MUST'VE GONE BACK AND FORTH FOR MONTHS.
BY
AN' I SAY 'TAINT!
I SAY 'TIS!
REMEMBER THAT, AMELIA? AMELIA?
OH, IGNORE HER, MR. McBRIDE. SHE'S ALWAYS GROUCHY IN THE MORNING.
Not this time! They're talking about me!
Oh, they're probably just talking about sports! They always disagree!
YEAH, I... I GUESS THAT'S IT.
What? Why would they be fighting about you? You're their favorite Chick!
WHAT'S THIS TOY?
HMMM? OH...THAT'S THE SOFTEE TALKIE.
I was complaining to the other chickens about our feed! I bet they overheard me, because they haven't stopped fighting since!
WE THOUGHT WALKIE-TALKIES WOULD BE A BIG HIT WITH KIDS.
FLIP
TILL WE REALIZED MOST OF 'EM HAVE CELL PHONES.
'Tis, ya dang Ronkwaller!
Dat 'taint eve a word!
WALKIE-TALKIES, EH? THEY COULD COME IN HANDY WITH MY CRIME FIGHTING.
Gosh, Softee! They sure are mad! What are you gonna do?
The only thing I can...
MY LAST SET WAS CONFISCATE BY SANTA CLAUS WHEN I TRIED TO BUST HIM.

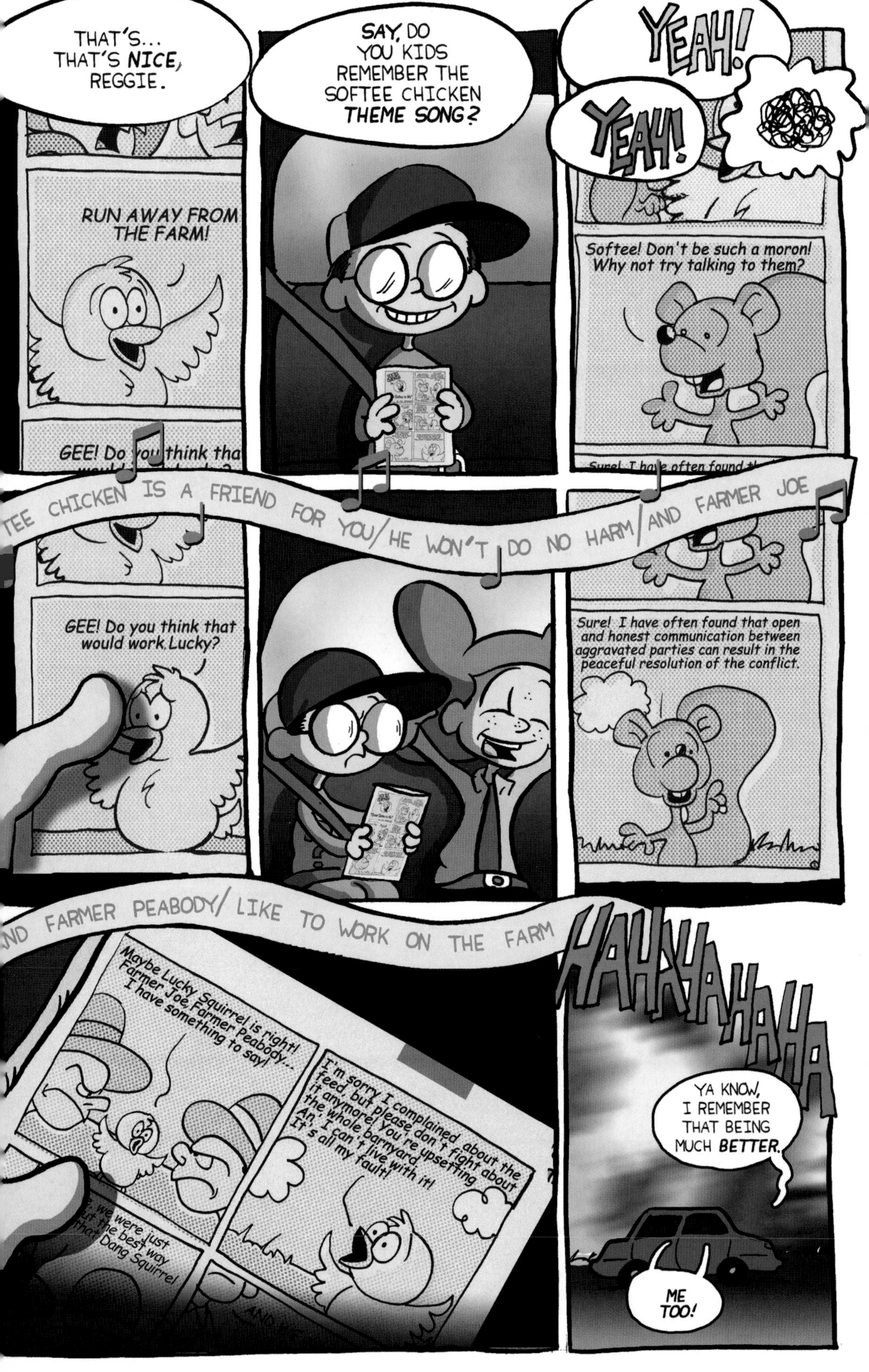

THAT'S... THAT'S NICE, REGGIE.
RUN AWAY FROM THE FARM!
SAY, DO YOU KIDS REMEMBER THE SOFTEE CHICKEN THEME SONG?
YEAH!
YEAH!
Softee! Don't be such a moron! Why not try talking to them?
TEE CHICKEN IS A FRIEND FOR YOU/ HE WON'T DO NO HARM/ AND FARMER JOE
GEE! Do you think that would work,Lucky?
Sure! I have often found that open and honest communication between aggravated parties can result in the peaceful resolution of the conflict.
ND FARMER PEABODY/ LIKE TO WORK ON THE FARM
Maybe Lucky Squirrel is right! Farmer Joe,Farmer Peabody... I have something to say!
I'm sorry I complained about the feed, but please don't fight about it anymore! You're upsetting the whole barnyard. An' I can't live with it! It's all my fault!
HAHAHAHAHAHA
YA KNOW, I REMEMBER THAT BEING MUCH BETTER.
ME TOO!

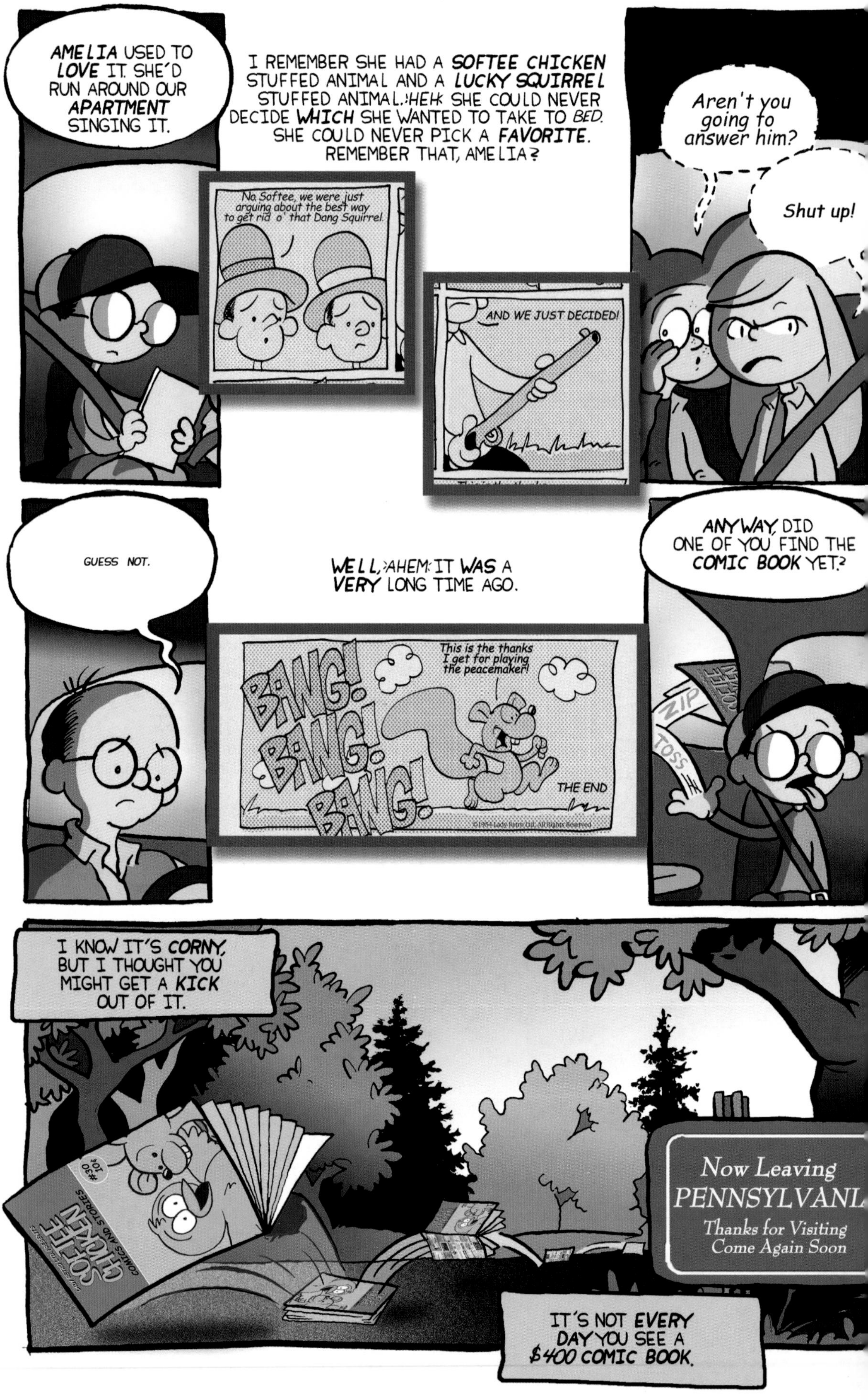
AMELIA USED TO LOVE IT. SHE'D RUN AROUND OUR APARTMENT SINGING IT.
I REMEMBER SHE HAD A SOFTEE CHICKEN STUFFED ANIMAL AND A LUCKY SQUIRREL STUFFED ANIMAL. *HEH* SHE COULD NEVER DECIDE WHICH SHE WANTED TO TAKE TO BED. SHE COULD NEVER PICK A FAVORITE. REMEMBER THAT, AMELIA?
No, Softee, we were just arguing about the best way to get rid o' that Dang Squirrel.
AND WE JUST DECIDED!
Aren't you going to answer him?
Shut up!
GUESS NOT.
WELL, *AHEM* IT WAS A VERY LONG TIME AGO.
BANG! BANG! BANG!
This is the thanks I get for playing the peacemaker!
THE END
ANYWAY, DID ONE OF YOU FIND THE COMIC BOOK YET?
ZIP
TOSS
SOFTEE CHICKEN
I KNOW IT'S CORNY, BUT I THOUGHT YOU MIGHT GET A KICK OUT OF IT.
SOFTEE CHICKEN
COMICS AND STORIES
#20
10¢
Now Leaving
PENNSYLVANI
Thanks for Visiting
Come Again Soon
IT'S NOT EVERY DAY YOU SEE A $400 COMIC BOOK.

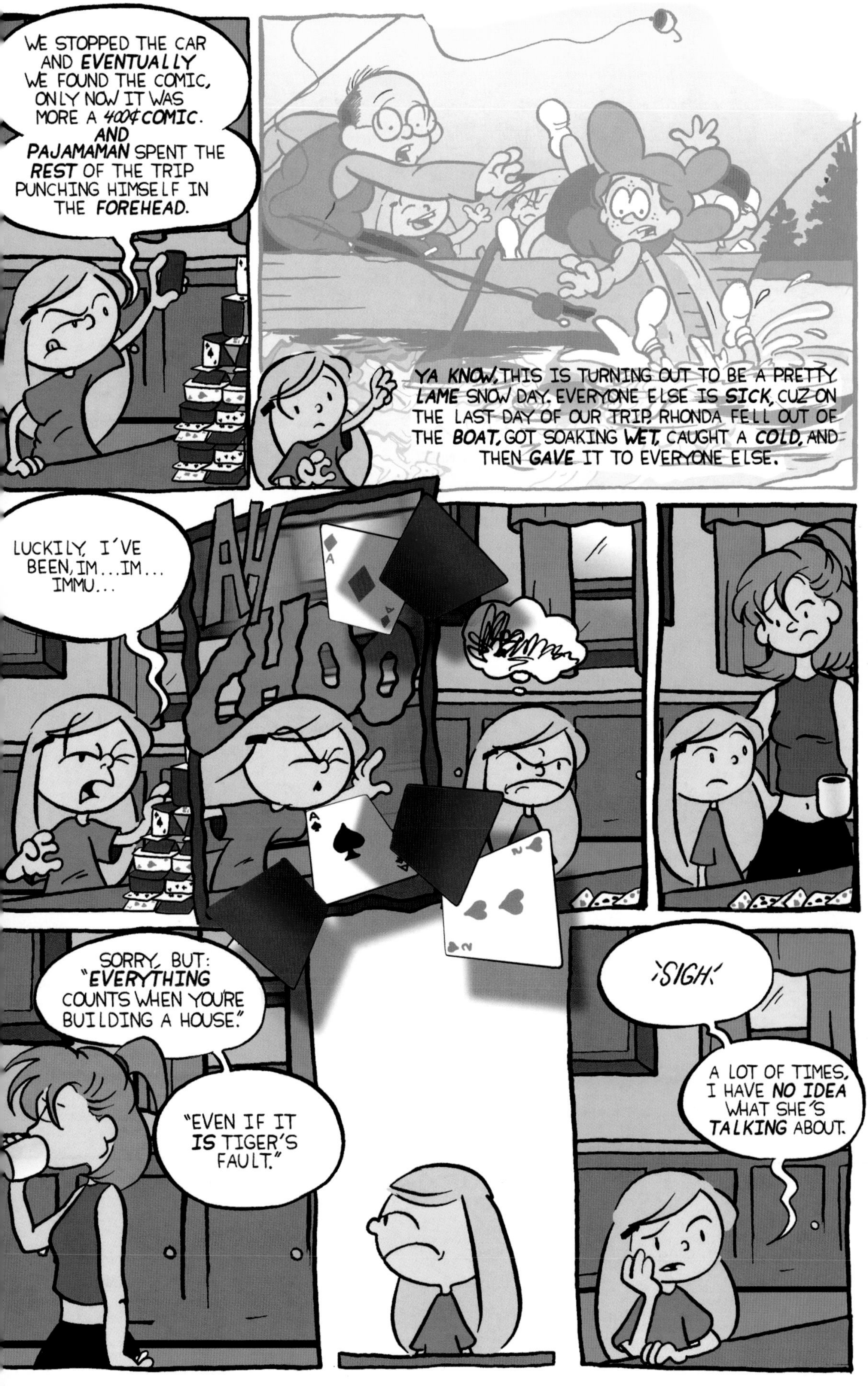
WE STOPPED THE CAR AND **EVENTUALLY** WE FOUND THE COMIC, ONLY NOW IT WAS MORE A *400¢* **COMIC.** **AND PAJAMAMAN** SPENT THE **REST** OF THE TRIP PUNCHING HIMSELF IN THE **FOREHEAD.**
YA KNOW, THIS IS TURNING OUT TO BE A PRETTY **LAME** SNOW DAY. EVERYONE ELSE IS **SICK,** CUZ ON THE LAST DAY OF OUR TRIP, RHONDA FELL OUT OF THE **BOAT,** GOT SOAKING **WET,** CAUGHT A **COLD,** AND THEN **GAVE** IT TO EVERYONE ELSE.
LUCKILY, I'VE BEEN, IM...IM... IMMU...
AH CHOO
SORRY, BUT: "**EVERYTHING** COUNTS WHEN YOU'RE BUILDING A HOUSE."
"EVEN IF IT **IS** TIGER'S FAULT."
:SIGH:
A LOT OF TIMES, I HAVE **NO IDEA** WHAT SHE'S **TALKING** ABOUT.

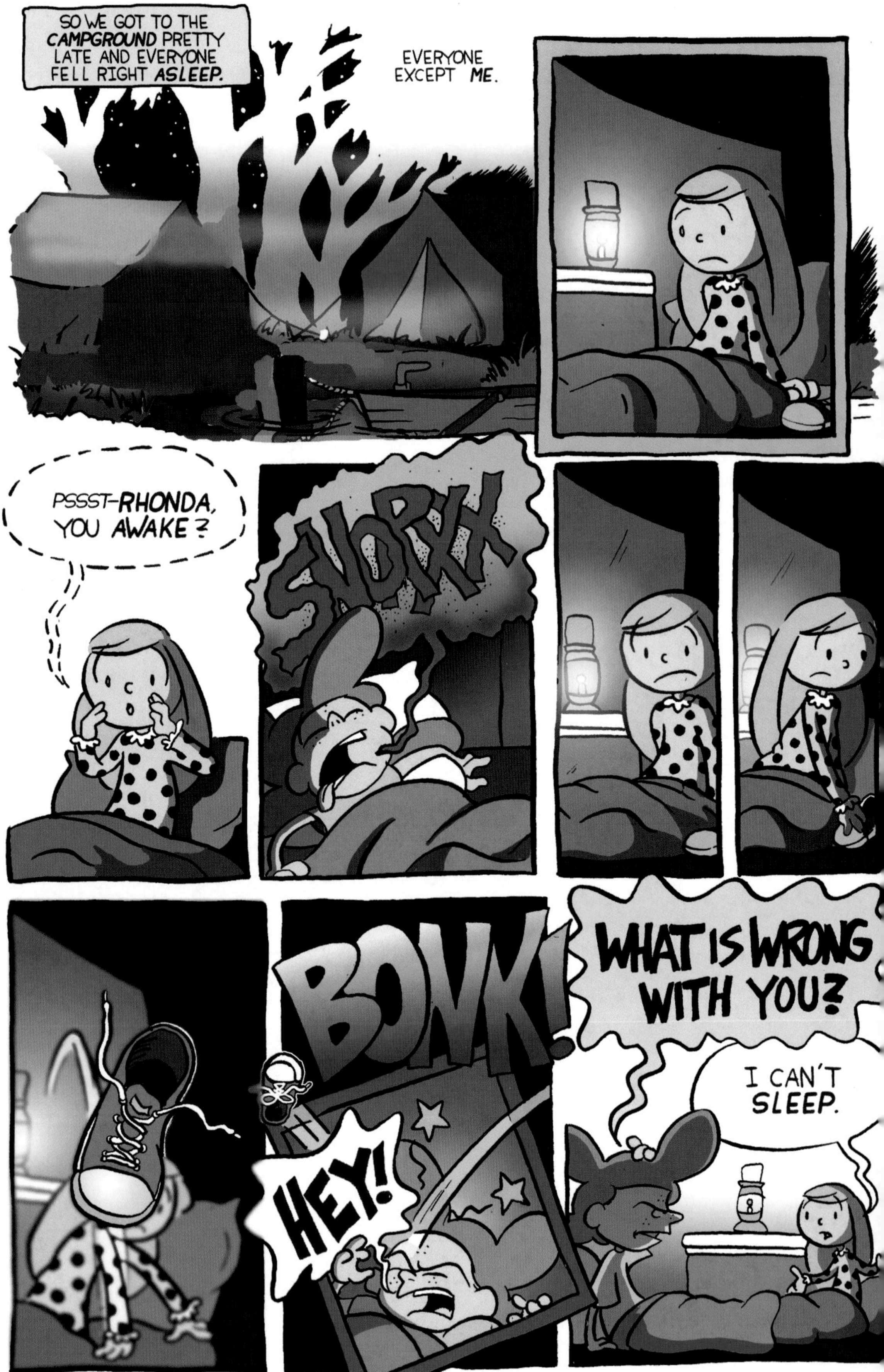
SO WE GOT TO THE CAMPGROUND PRETTY LATE AND EVERYONE FELL RIGHT ASLEEP.
EVERYONE EXCEPT ME.
PSSST-RHONDA, YOU AWAKE?
SNORKK
BONK!
HEY!
WHAT IS WRONG WITH YOU?
I CAN'T SLEEP.

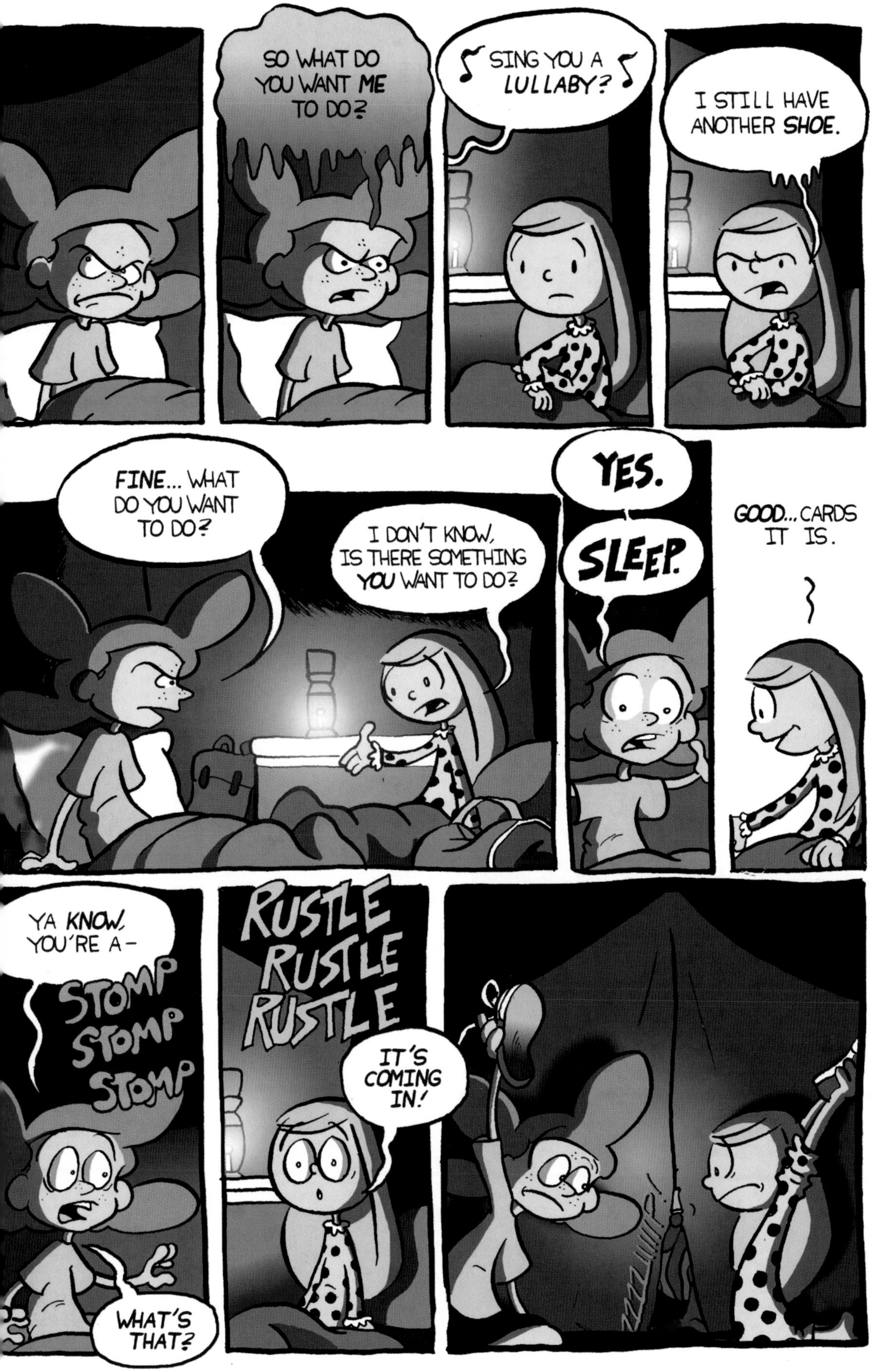
SO WHAT DO YOU WANT **ME** TO DO?
SING YOU A **LULLABY**?
I STILL HAVE ANOTHER **SHOE**.
FINE... WHAT DO YOU WANT TO DO?
I DON'T KNOW, IS THERE SOMETHING **YOU** WANT TO DO?
YES.
SLEEP.
GOOD... CARDS IT IS.
YA **KNOW**, YOU'RE A-
STOMP STOMP STOMP
WHAT'S THAT?
RUSTLE RUSTLE RUSTLE
IT'S COMING IN!
ZZZZIIIIIIP!

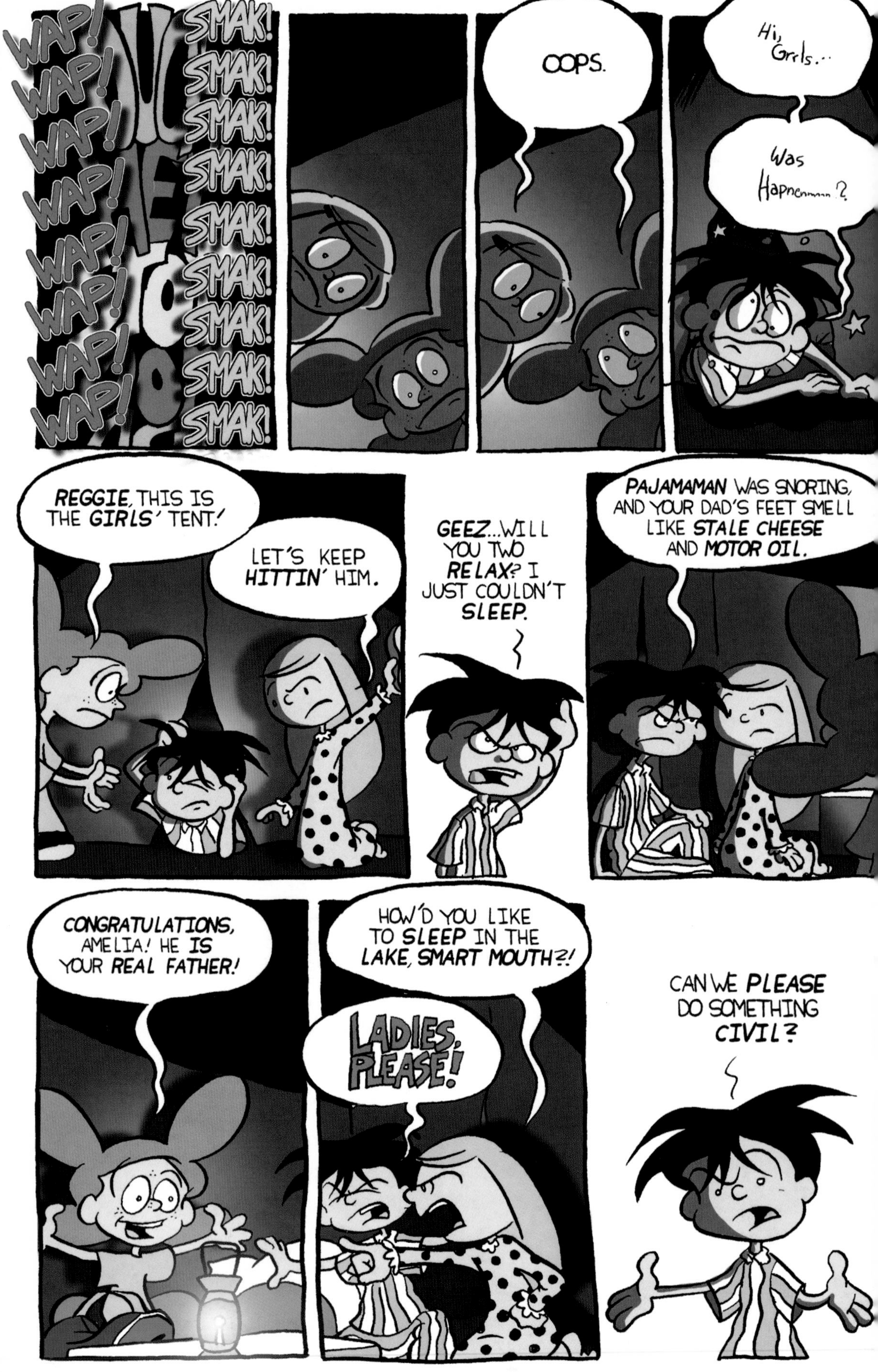
WAP! WAP! WAP! WAP! WAP! WAP! WAP! WAP!
SMAK! SMAK! SMAK! SMAK! SMAK! SMAK! SMAK! SMAK! SMAK!
OOPS.
Hi, Grrls...
Was Hapnennnn?
REGGIE, THIS IS THE GIRLS' TENT!
LET'S KEEP HITTIN' HIM.
GEEZ...WILL YOU TWO RELAX? I JUST COULDN'T SLEEP.
PAJAMAMAN WAS SNORING, AND YOUR DAD'S FEET SMELL LIKE STALE CHEESE AND MOTOR OIL.
CONGRATULATIONS, AMELIA! HE IS YOUR REAL FATHER!
HOW'D YOU LIKE TO SLEEP IN THE LAKE, SMART MOUTH?!
LADIES, PLEASE!
CAN WE PLEASE DO SOMETHING CIVIL?

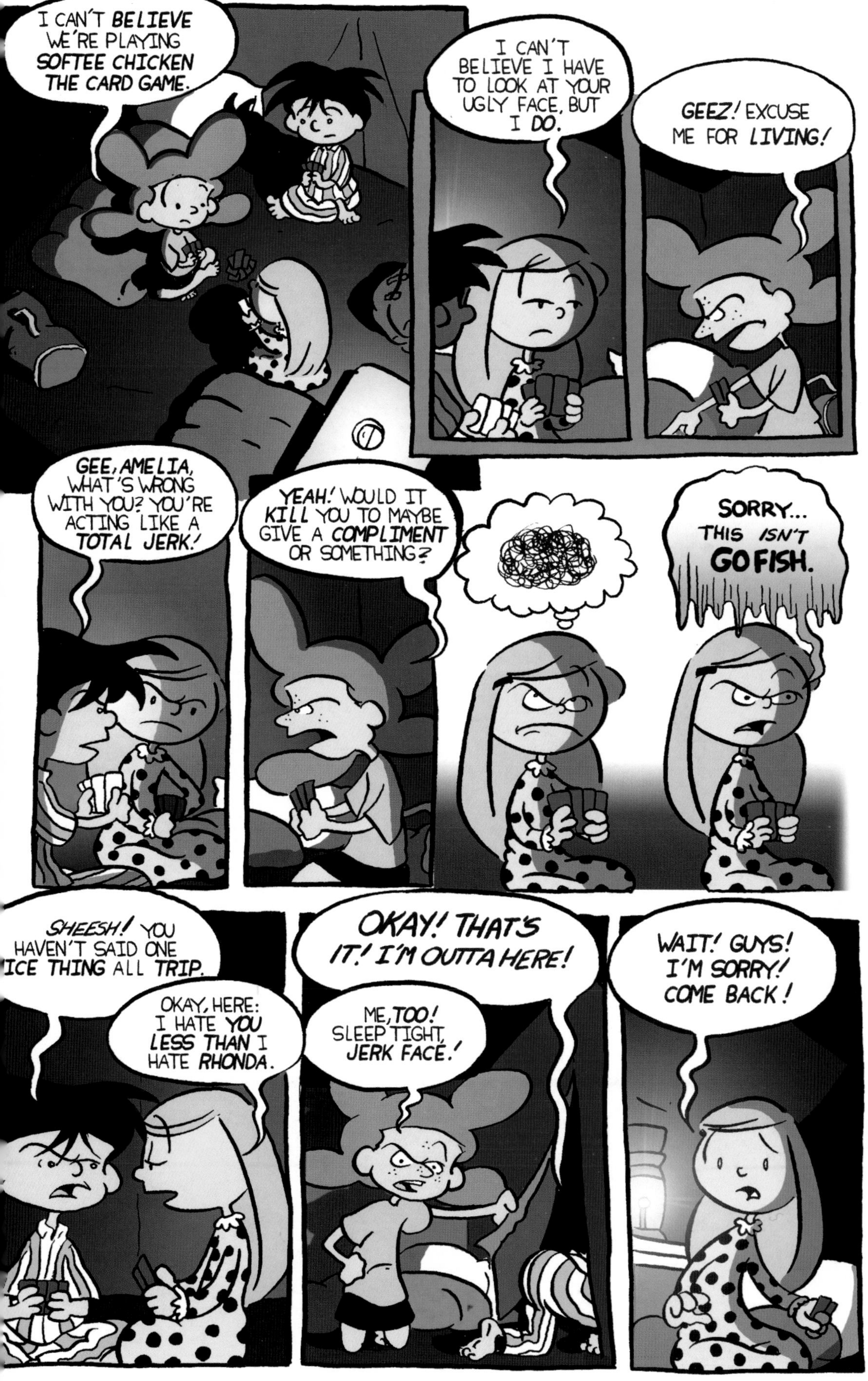

I CAN'T BELIEVE WE'RE PLAYING SOFTEE CHICKEN THE CARD GAME.
I CAN'T BELIEVE I HAVE TO LOOK AT YOUR UGLY FACE, BUT I DO.
GEEZ! EXCUSE ME FOR LIVING!
GEE, AMELIA, WHAT'S WRONG WITH YOU? YOU'RE ACTING LIKE A TOTAL JERK!
YEAH! WOULD IT KILL YOU TO MAYBE GIVE A COMPLIMENT OR SOMETHING?
SORRY... THIS ISN'T GO FISH.
SHEESH! YOU HAVEN'T SAID ONE ICE THING ALL TRIP.
OKAY, HERE: I HATE YOU LESS THAN I HATE RHONDA.
OKAY! THAT'S IT! I'M OUTTA HERE!
ME, TOO! SLEEP TIGHT, JERK FACE!
WAIT! GUYS! I'M SORRY! COME BACK!

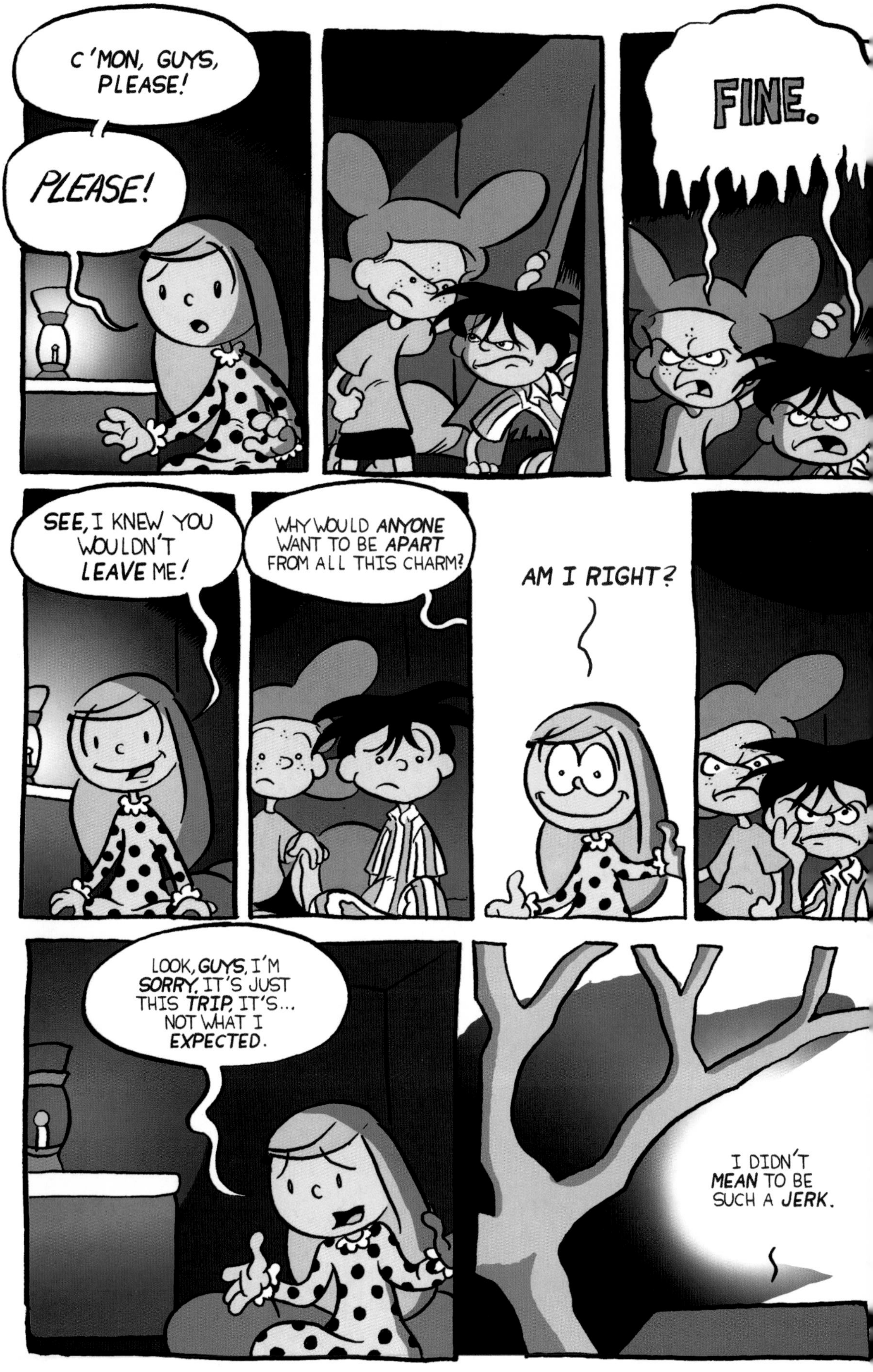
C'MON, GUYS, PLEASE!
PLEASE!
FINE.
SEE, I KNEW YOU WOULDN'T LEAVE ME!
WHY WOULD ANYONE WANT TO BE APART FROM ALL THIS CHARM?
AM I RIGHT?
LOOK, GUYS, I'M SORRY. IT'S JUST THIS TRIP, IT'S... NOT WHAT I EXPECTED.
I DIDN'T MEAN TO BE SUCH A JERK.

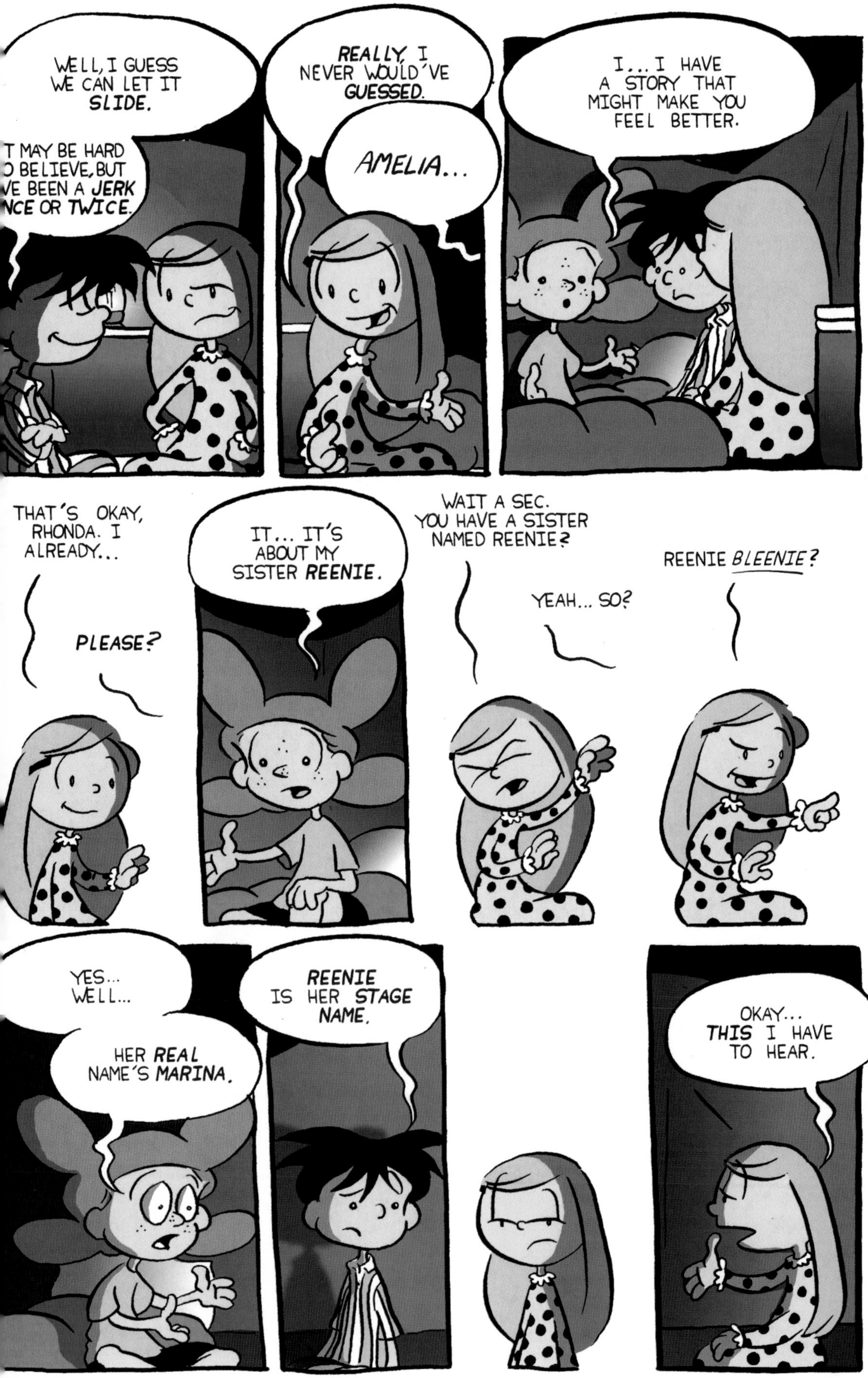
WELL, I GUESS WE CAN LET IT SLIDE.
T MAY BE HARD) BELIEVE, BUT VE BEEN A JERK NCE OR TWICE.
REALLY. I NEVER WOULD'VE GUESSED.
AMELIA...
I... I HAVE A STORY THAT MIGHT MAKE YOU FEEL BETTER.
THAT'S OKAY, RHONDA. I ALREADY...
PLEASE?
IT... IT'S ABOUT MY SISTER REENIE.
WAIT A SEC. YOU HAVE A SISTER NAMED REENIE?
YEAH... SO?
REENIE BLEENIE?
YES... WELL...
HER REAL NAME'S MARINA.
REENIE IS HER STAGE NAME.
OKAY... THIS I HAVE TO HEAR.

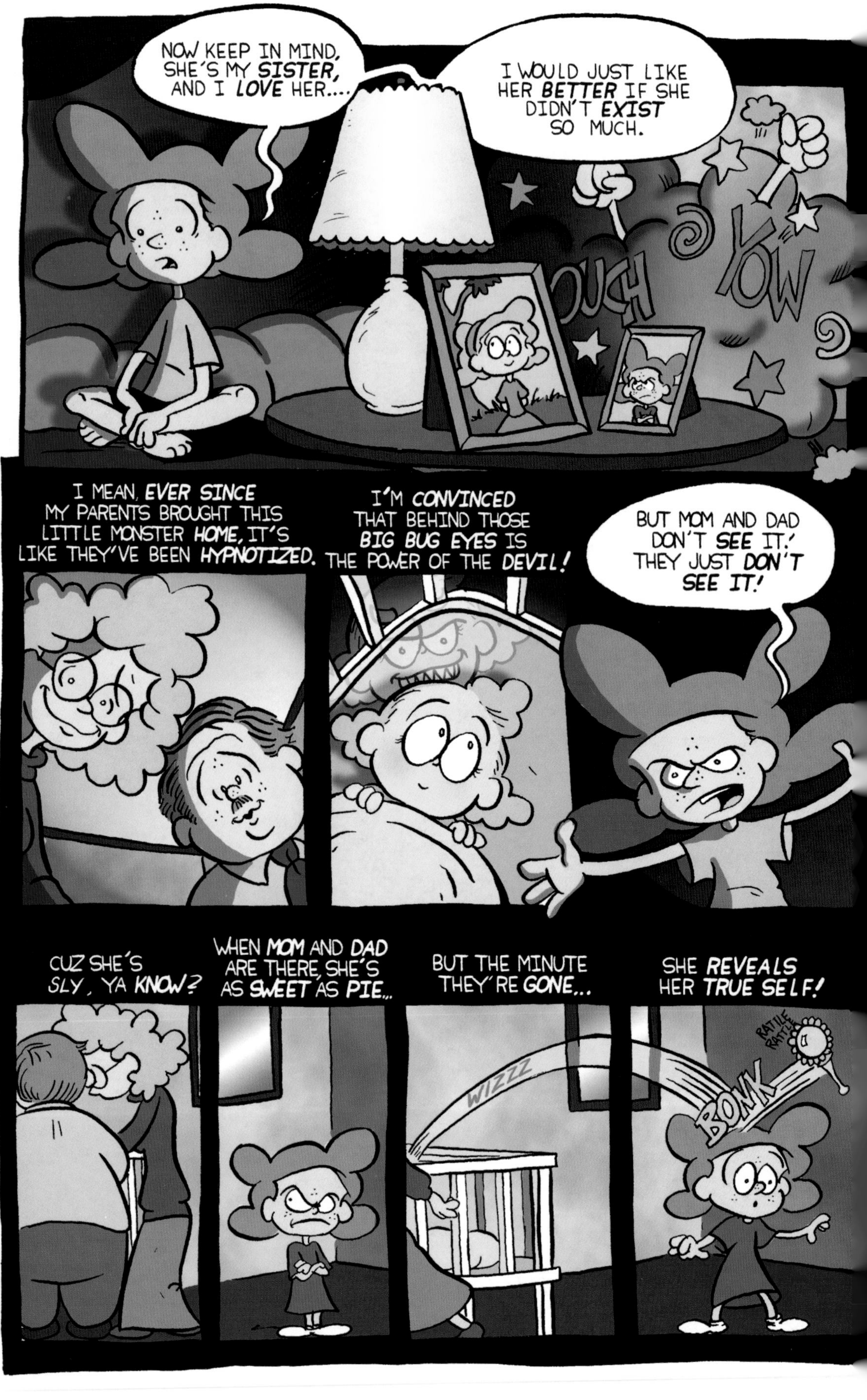
NOW KEEP IN MIND, SHE'S MY SISTER, AND I LOVE HER....
I WOULD JUST LIKE HER BETTER IF SHE DIDN'T EXIST SO MUCH.
OUCH
YOW
I MEAN, EVER SINCE MY PARENTS BROUGHT THIS LITTLE MONSTER HOME, IT'S LIKE THEY'VE BEEN HYPNOTIZED.
I'M CONVINCED THAT BEHIND THOSE BIG BUG EYES IS THE POWER OF THE DEVIL!
BUT MOM AND DAD DON'T SEE IT! THEY JUST DON'T SEE IT!
CUZ SHE'S SLY, YA KNOW?
WHEN MOM AND DAD ARE THERE, SHE'S AS SWEET AS PIE...
BUT THE MINUTE THEY'RE GONE...
WIZZZ
SHE REVEALS HER TRUE SELF!
RATTLE RATTLE
BONK

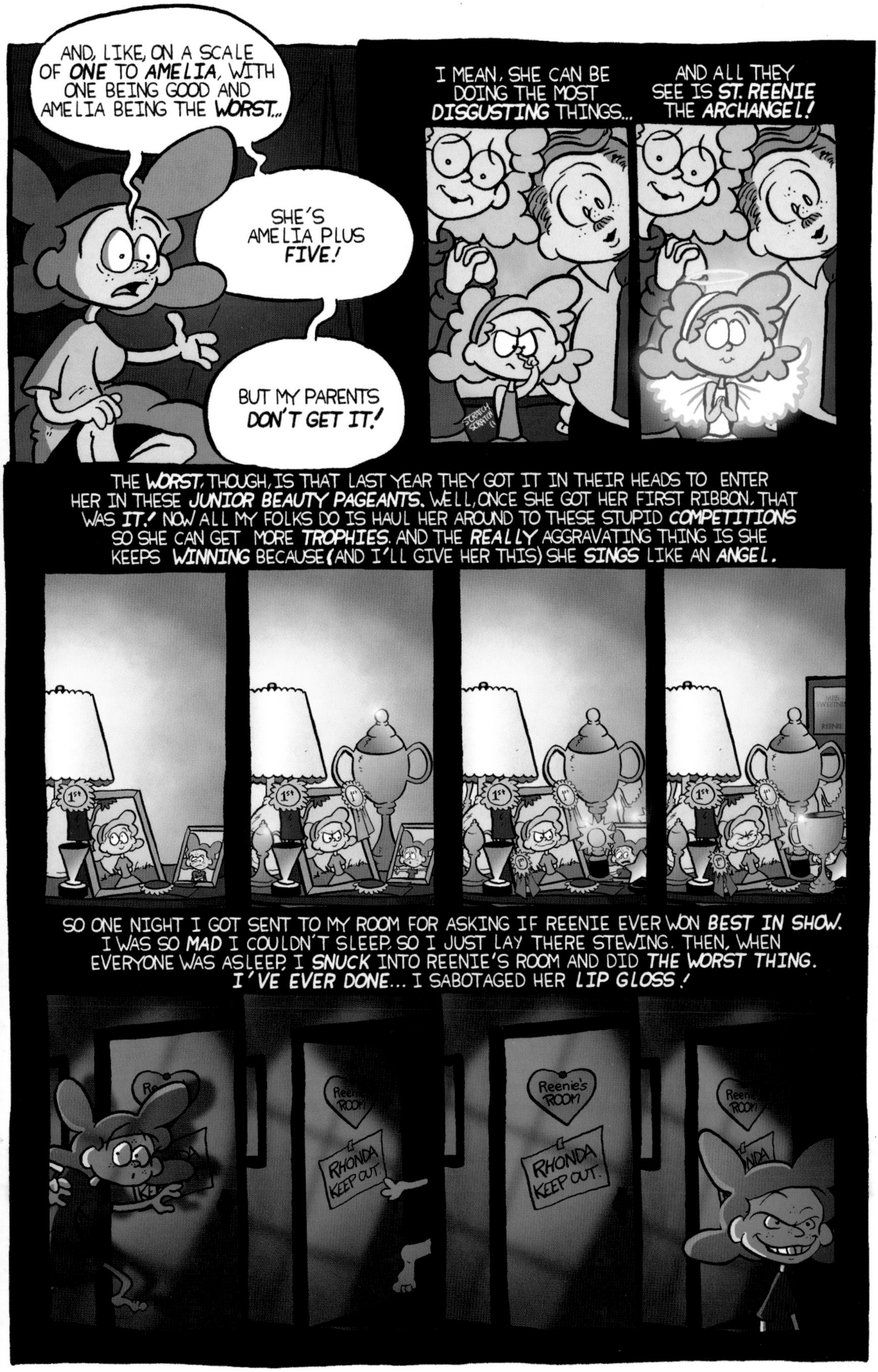
AND, LIKE, ON A SCALE OF ONE TO AMELIA, WITH ONE BEING GOOD AND AMELIA BEING THE WORST...
SHE'S AMELIA PLUS FIVE!
BUT MY PARENTS DON'T GET IT!
I MEAN, SHE CAN BE DOING THE MOST DISGUSTING THINGS...
SCRATCH SCRATCH
AND ALL THEY SEE IS ST. REENIE THE ARCHANGEL!
THE WORST, THOUGH, IS THAT LAST YEAR THEY GOT IT IN THEIR HEADS TO ENTER HER IN THESE JUNIOR BEAUTY PAGEANTS. WELL, ONCE SHE GOT HER FIRST RIBBON, THAT WAS IT! NOW ALL MY FOLKS DO IS HAUL HER AROUND TO THESE STUPID COMPETITIONS SO SHE CAN GET MORE TROPHIES. AND THE REALLY AGGRAVATING THING IS SHE KEEPS WINNING BECAUSE (AND I'LL GIVE HER THIS) SHE SINGS LIKE AN ANGEL.
SO ONE NIGHT I GOT SENT TO MY ROOM FOR ASKING IF REENIE EVER WON BEST IN SHOW. I WAS SO MAD I COULDN'T SLEEP, SO I JUST LAY THERE STEWING. THEN, WHEN EVERYONE WAS ASLEEP, I SNUCK INTO REENIE'S ROOM AND DID THE WORST THING. I'VE EVER DONE... I SABOTAGED HER LIP GLOSS!
Reenie's ROOM
RHONDA KEEP OUT.

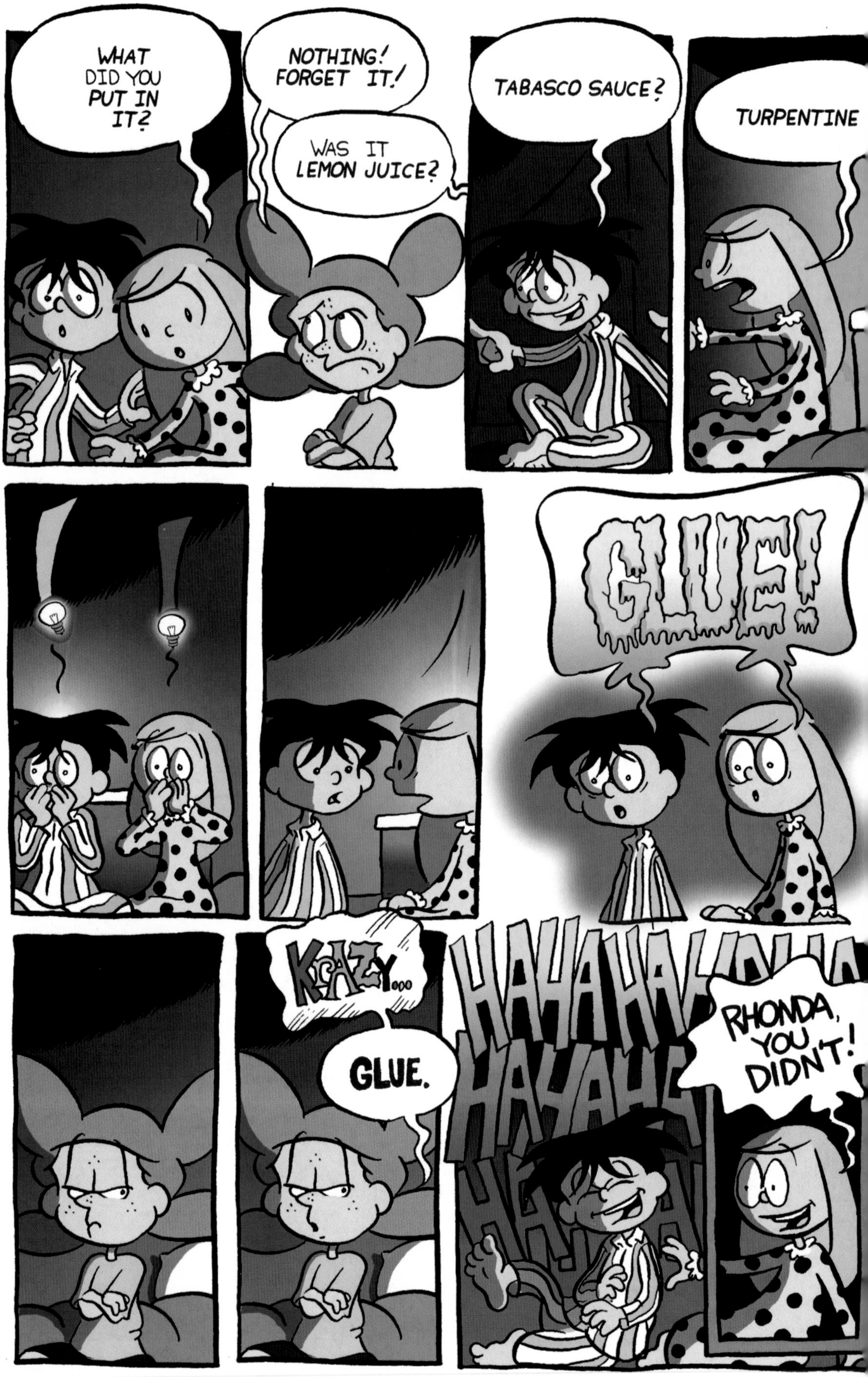

WHAT DID YOU PUT IN IT?
NOTHING! FORGET IT!
WAS IT LEMON JUICE?
TABASCO SAUCE?
TURPENTINE
GLUE!
KRAZY...
GLUE.
HAHAHAHA HAHAHA
RHONDA, YOU DIDN'T!

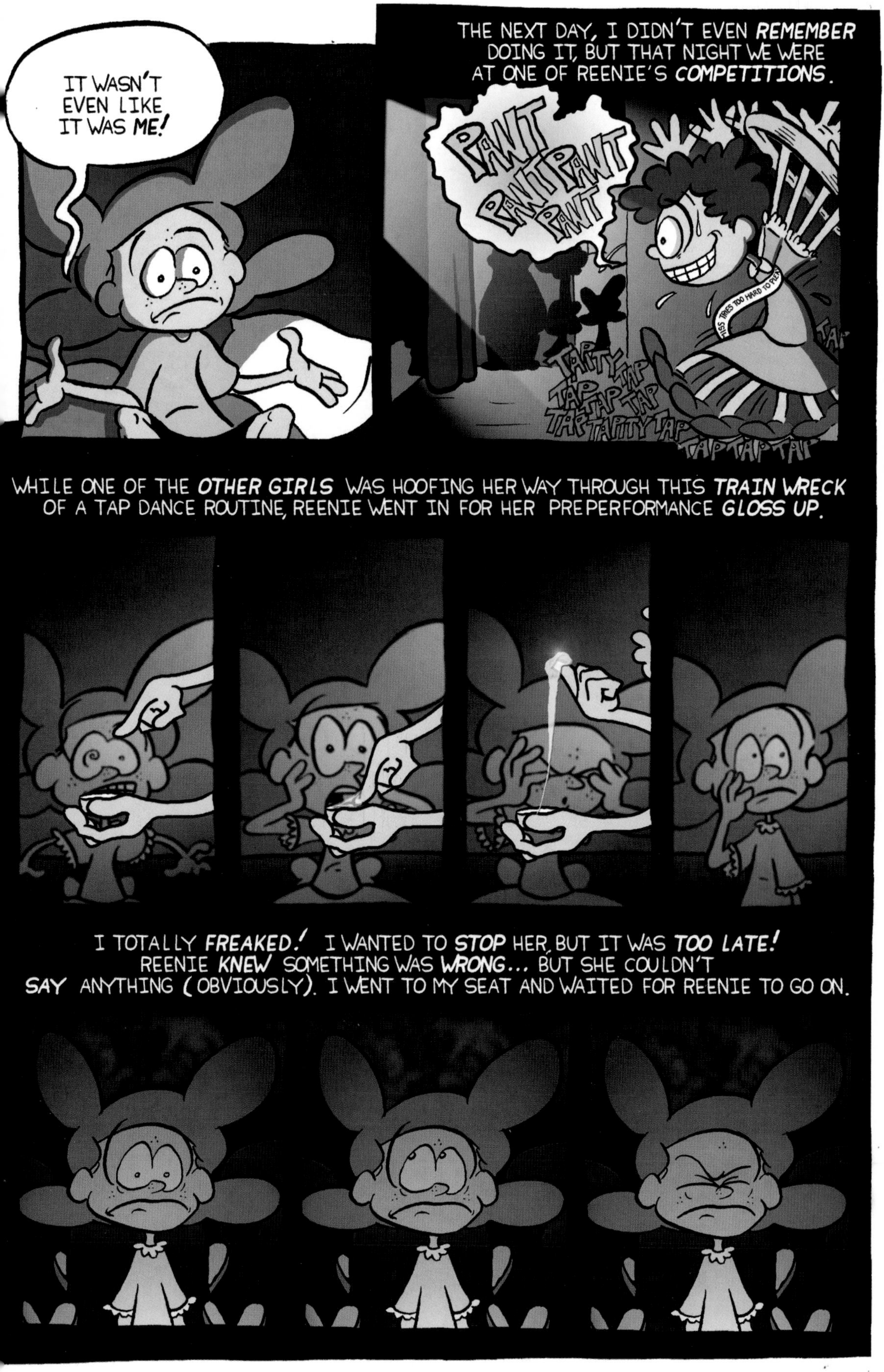

IT WASN'T EVEN LIKE IT WAS ME!
THE NEXT DAY, I DIDN'T EVEN REMEMBER DOING IT, BUT THAT NIGHT WE WERE AT ONE OF REENIE'S COMPETITIONS.
PANT PANT PANT PANT PANT
TRIES TOO HARD TO
TAPPITY TAP TAP TAP TAP TAP TAP TAPPITY TAP
TAP TAP TAP
WHILE ONE OF THE OTHER GIRLS WAS HOOFING HER WAY THROUGH THIS TRAIN WRECK OF A TAP DANCE ROUTINE, REENIE WENT IN FOR HER PREPERFORMANCE GLOSS UP.
I TOTALLY FREAKED! I WANTED TO STOP HER, BUT IT WAS TOO LATE! REENIE KNEW SOMETHING WAS WRONG... BUT SHE COULDN'T SAY ANYTHING (OBVIOUSLY). I WENT TO MY SEAT AND WAITED FOR REENIE TO GO ON.

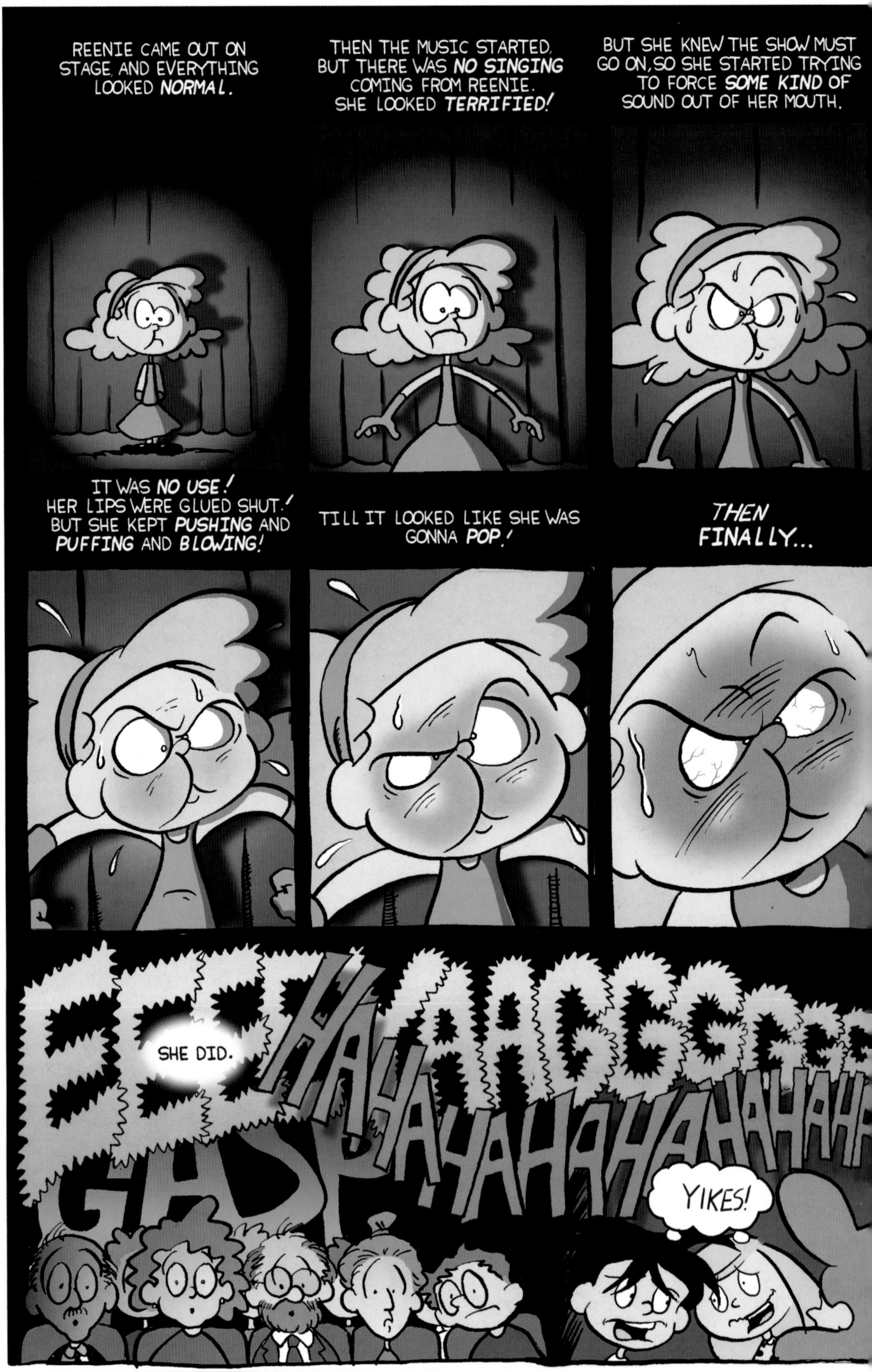

REENIE CAME OUT ON STAGE, AND EVERYTHING LOOKED **NORMAL**.
THEN THE MUSIC STARTED, BUT THERE WAS **NO SINGING** COMING FROM REENIE. SHE LOOKED **TERRIFIED!**
BUT SHE KNEW THE SHOW MUST GO ON, SO SHE STARTED TRYING TO FORCE **SOME KIND OF** SOUND OUT OF HER MOUTH.
IT WAS **NO USE!** HER LIPS WERE GLUED SHUT! BUT SHE KEPT **PUSHING** AND **PUFFING** AND **BLOWING!**
TILL IT LOOKED LIKE SHE WAS GONNA **POP!**
THEN **FINALLY...**
SHE DID.
HAHAHAHAHAHAHAHAHAH
GASP!
YIKES!

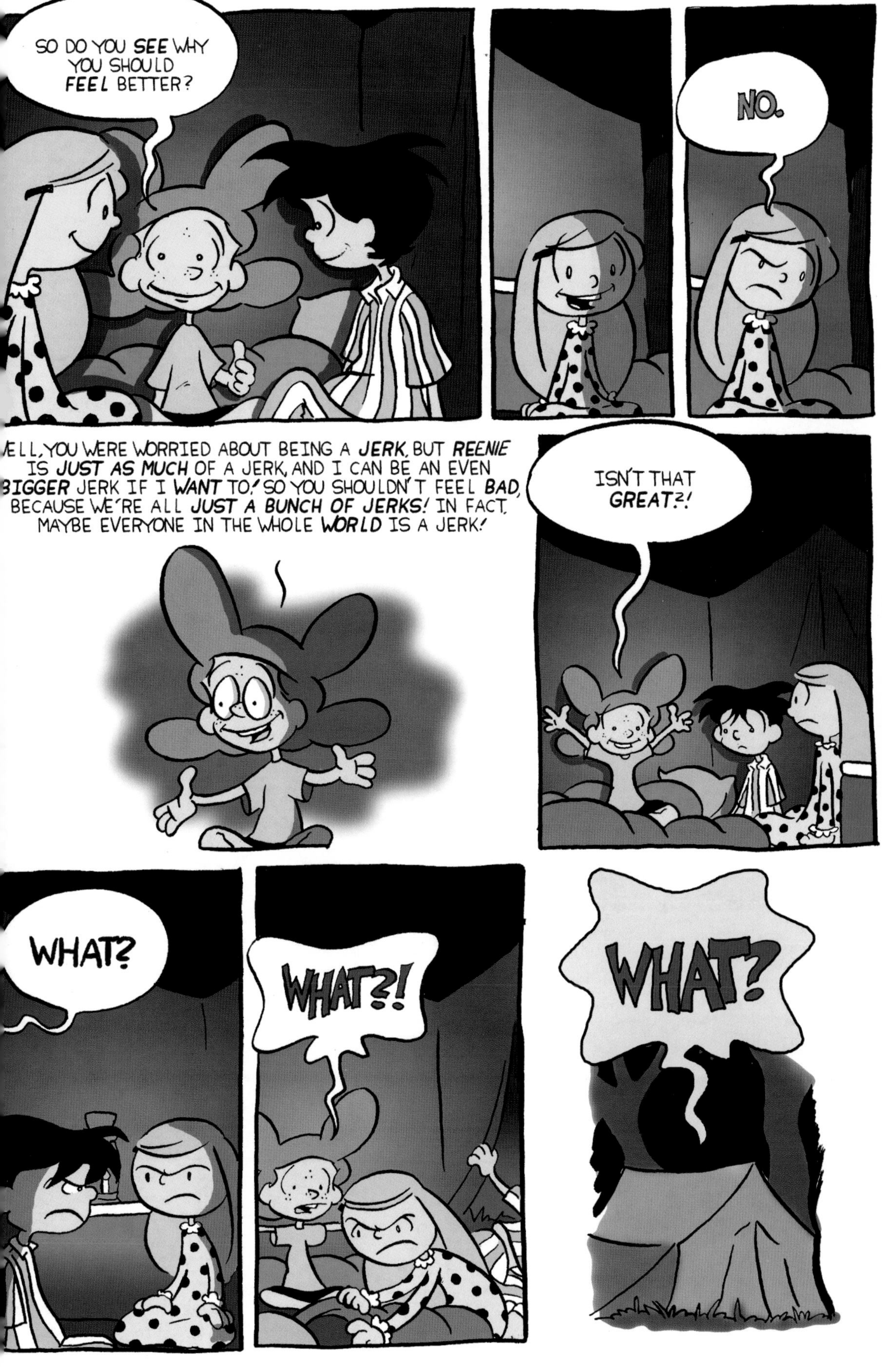
SO DO YOU SEE WHY YOU SHOULD FEEL BETTER?
NO.
ELL, YOU WERE WORRIED ABOUT BEING A JERK, BUT REENIE IS JUST AS MUCH OF A JERK, AND I CAN BE AN EVEN BIGGER JERK IF I WANT TO! SO YOU SHOULDN'T FEEL BAD, BECAUSE WE'RE ALL JUST A BUNCH OF JERKS! IN FACT, MAYBE EVERYONE IN THE WHOLE WORLD IS A JERK!
ISN'T THAT GREAT?!
WHAT?
WHAT?!
WHAT?

RHONDA'S STORY DIDN'T REALLY MAKE ME *FEEL BETTER,* IT PRETTY MUCH JUST *CREEPED ME OUT.*

SO I JUST SAT UP *ALL NIGHT* GETTING MORE AND MORE *MISERABLE.*

HOOSH

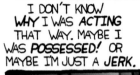

I DON'T KNOW *WHY* I WAS *ACTING* THAT WAY. MAYBE I WAS *POSSESSED!* OR MAYBE I'M JUST A *JERK.*

I MEAN, I LOVE MY *DAD* AND ALL, IT'S *JUST...*HMM... IT'S HARD WRITING *BACKWARD!*

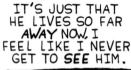

IT'S JUST THAT HE LIVES SO FAR *AWAY* NOW, I FEEL LIKE I NEVER GET TO *SEE* HIM.

SO WHEN I *DO* SEE HIM, I WANT IT TO JUST BE THE *TWO* OF US.

AAH, I *KNOW!* I *KNOW!* I'M A *SELFISH BRAT!* IT'S NOT MY *DAD'S* FAULT.

MAYBE IT'S BECAUSE I'M AN *ONLY CHILD.*

WHICH I GUESS *TECHNICALLY* PUTS THE BLAME BACK ON HIM AND *MOM.*

HMMM... YA KNOW, I *KINDA* FEEL BETTER *ALREADY.*

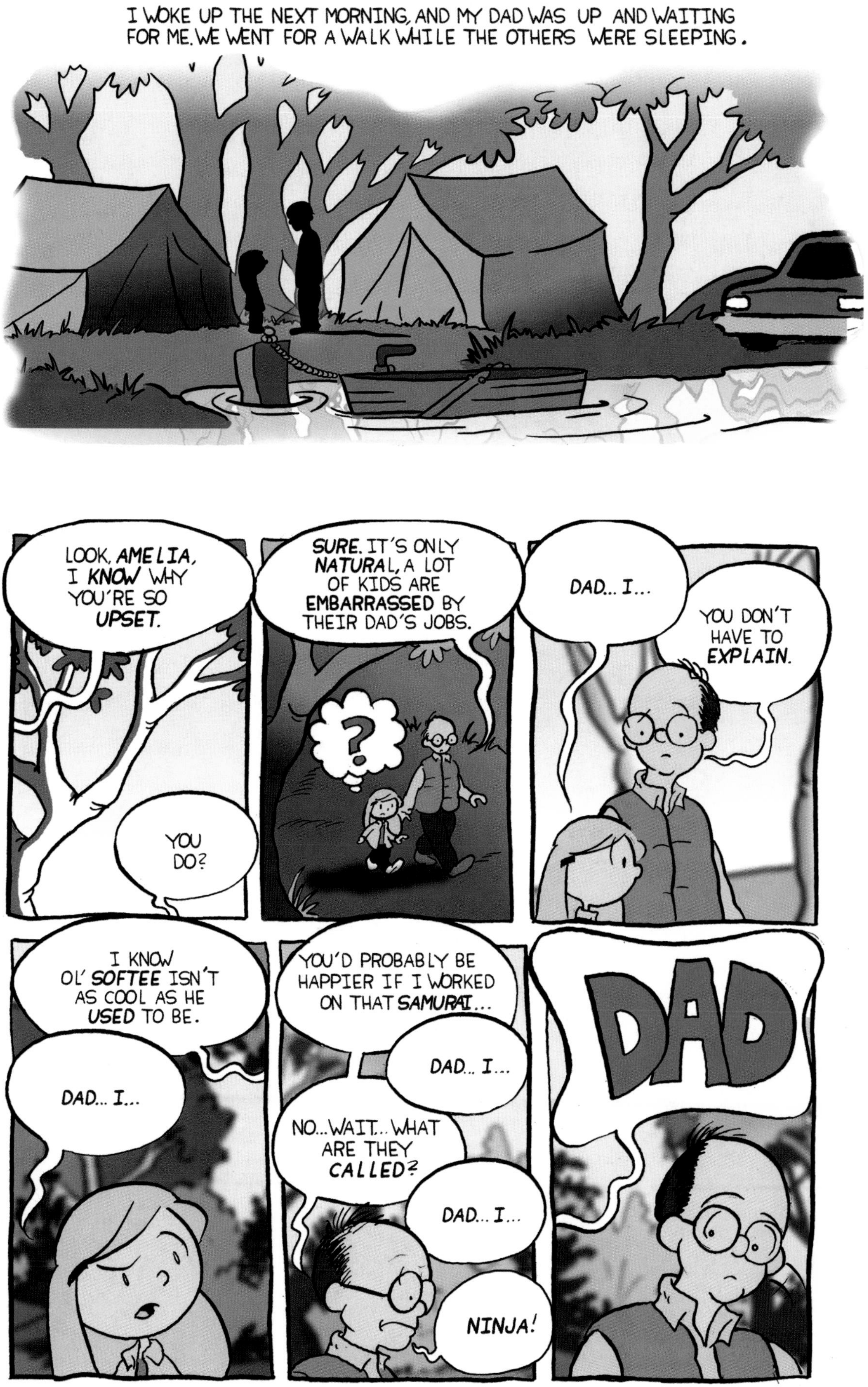
I WOKE UP THE NEXT MORNING, AND MY DAD WAS UP AND WAITING FOR ME. WE WENT FOR A WALK WHILE THE OTHERS WERE SLEEPING.
LOOK, AMELIA, I KNOW WHY YOU'RE SO UPSET.
YOU DO?
SURE. IT'S ONLY NATURAL, A LOT OF KIDS ARE EMBARRASSED BY THEIR DAD'S JOBS.
?
DAD... I...
YOU DON'T HAVE TO EXPLAIN.
I KNOW OL' SOFTEE ISN'T AS COOL AS HE USED TO BE.
DAD... I...
YOU'D PROBABLY BE HAPPIER IF I WORKED ON THAT SAMURAI...
DAD... I...
NO...WAIT... WHAT ARE THEY CALLED?
DAD... I...
NINJA!
DAD

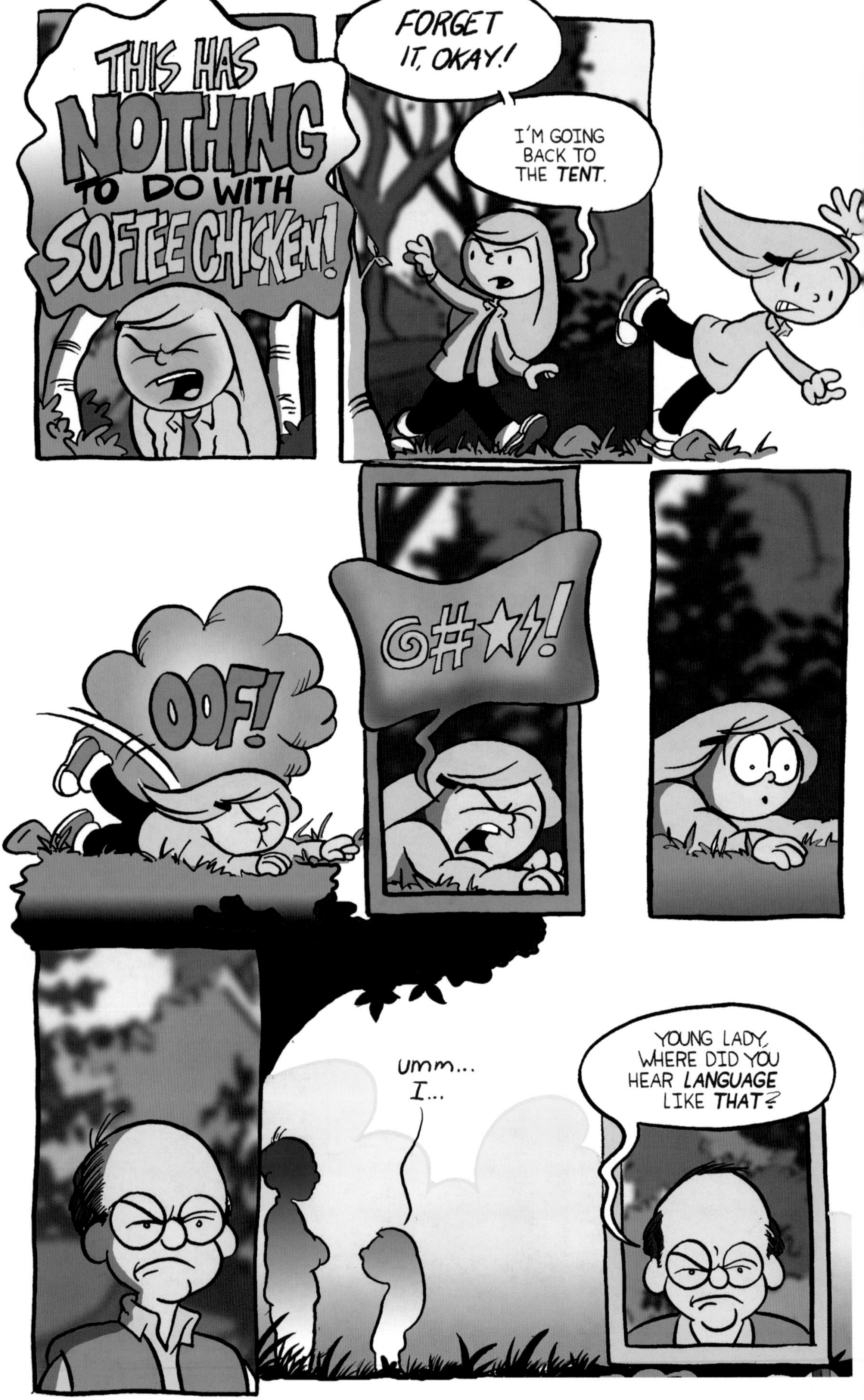
THIS HAS NOTHING TO DO WITH SOFTEE CHICKEN!
FORGET IT, OKAY!
I'M GOING BACK TO THE TENT.
OOF!
@#★ϟ!
umm... I...
YOUNG LADY, WHERE DID YOU HEAR LANGUAGE LIKE THAT?

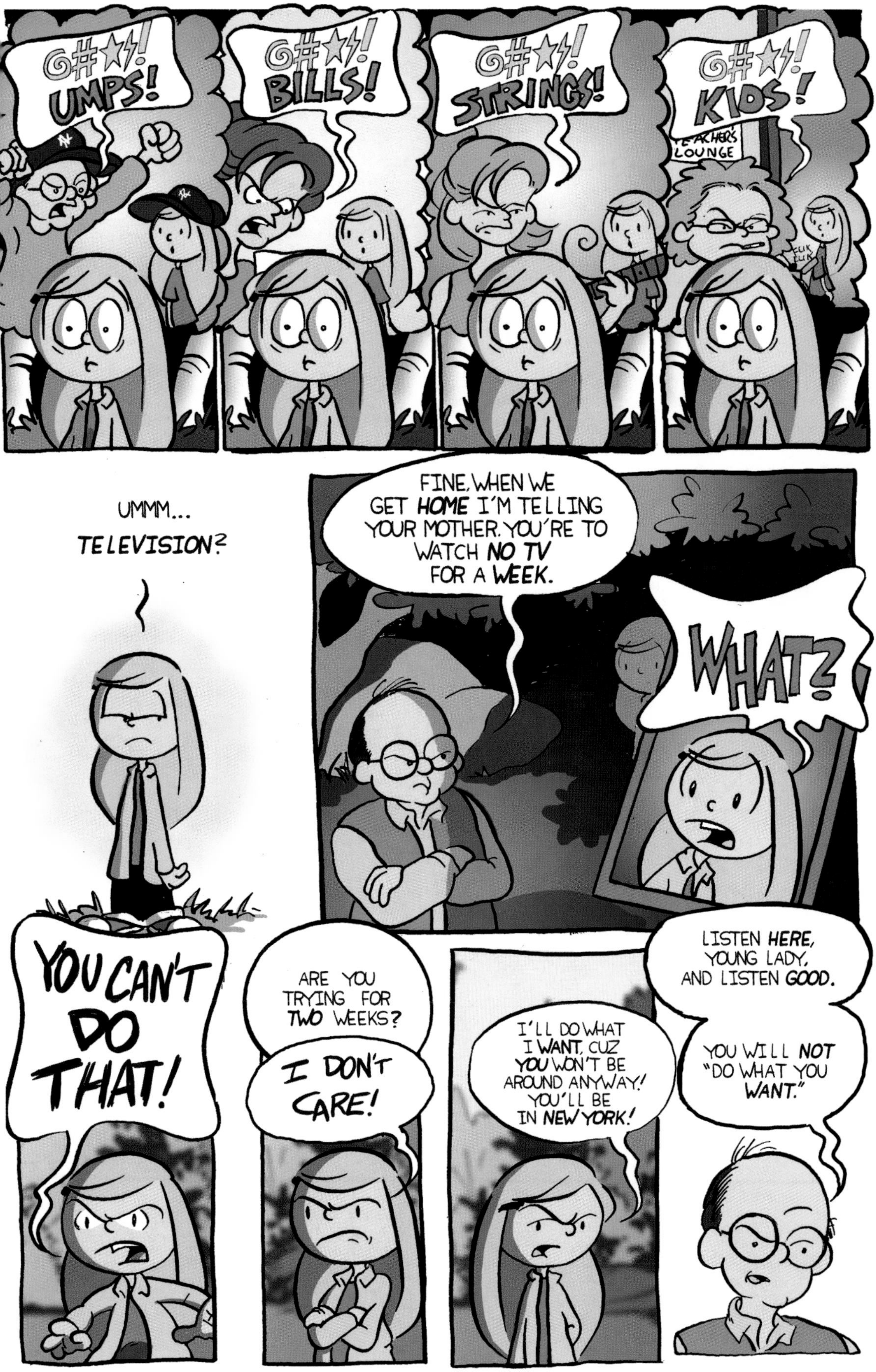

G#☆$! UMPS!
G#☆$! BILLS!
G#☆$! STRINGS!
G#☆$! KIDS!
TEACHER'S LOUNGE
UMMM... TELEVISION?
FINE, WHEN WE GET HOME I'M TELLING YOUR MOTHER. YOU'RE TO WATCH NO TV FOR A WEEK.
WHAT?!
YOU CAN'T DO THAT!
ARE YOU TRYING FOR TWO WEEKS?
I DON'T CARE!
I'LL DO WHAT I WANT, CUZ YOU WON'T BE AROUND ANYWAY! YOU'LL BE IN NEW YORK!
LISTEN HERE, YOUNG LADY, AND LISTEN GOOD.
YOU WILL NOT "DO WHAT YOU WANT."

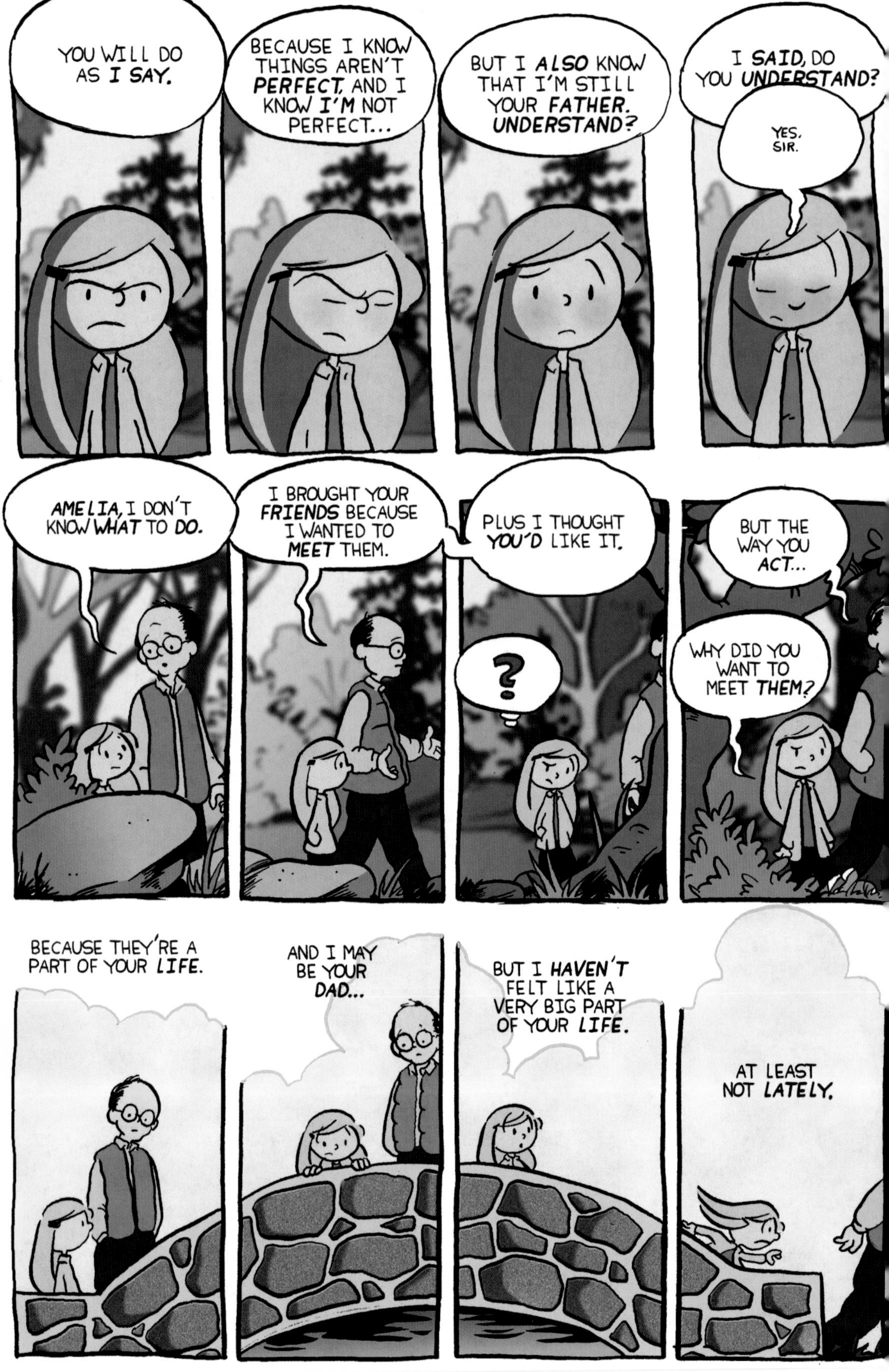
YOU WILL DO AS I SAY.
BECAUSE I KNOW THINGS AREN'T PERFECT, AND I KNOW I'M NOT PERFECT...
BUT I ALSO KNOW THAT I'M STILL YOUR FATHER. UNDERSTAND?
I SAID, DO YOU UNDERSTAND?
YES, SIR.
AMELIA, I DON'T KNOW WHAT TO DO.
I BROUGHT YOUR FRIENDS BECAUSE I WANTED TO MEET THEM.
PLUS I THOUGHT YOU'D LIKE IT.
?
BUT THE WAY YOU ACT...
WHY DID YOU WANT TO MEET THEM?
BECAUSE THEY'RE A PART OF YOUR LIFE.
AND I MAY BE YOUR DAD...
BUT I HAVEN'T FELT LIKE A VERY BIG PART OF YOUR LIFE.
AT LEAST NOT LATELY.

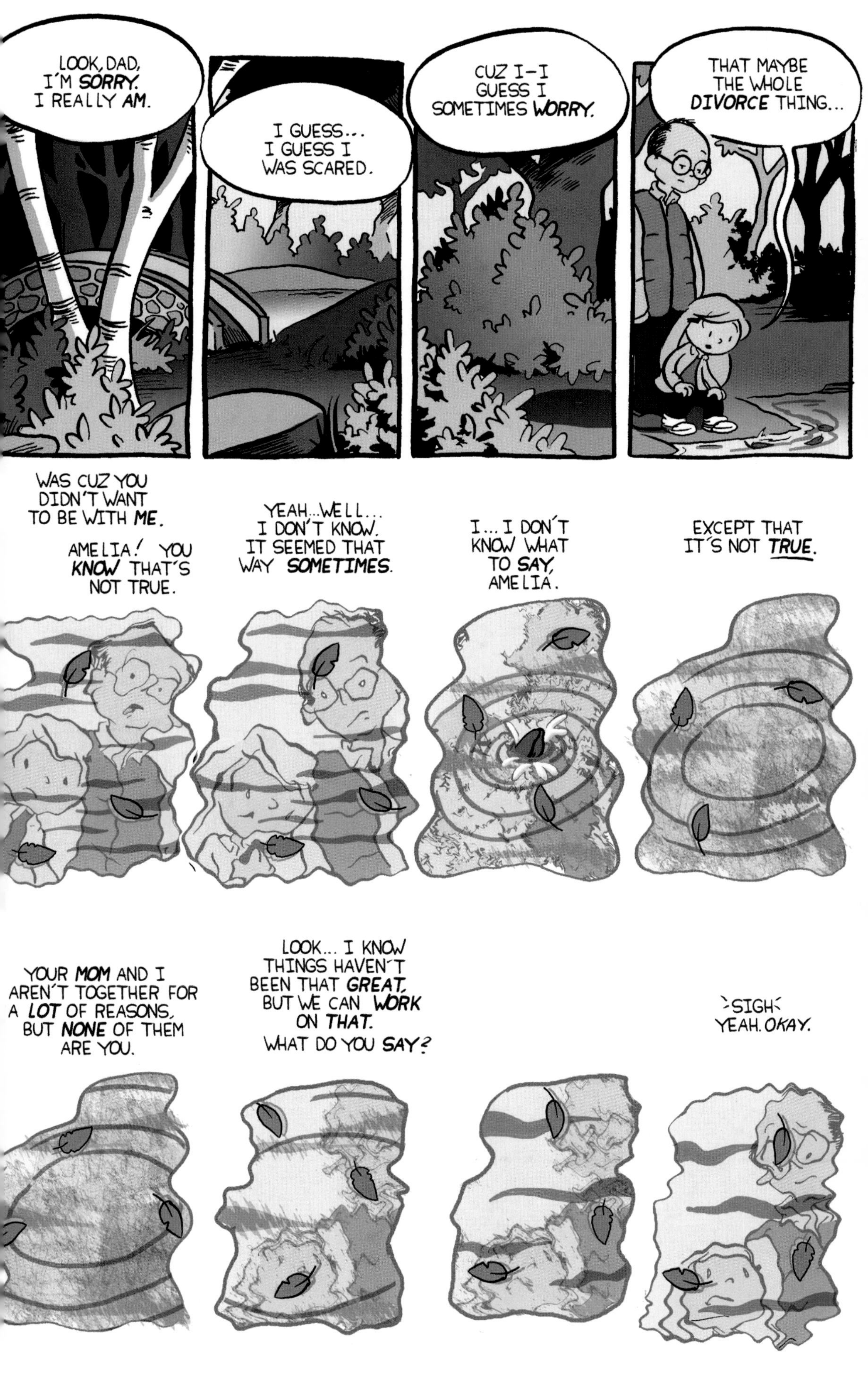
LOOK, DAD, I'M SORRY. I REALLY AM.
I GUESS... I GUESS I WAS SCARED.
CUZ I-I GUESS I SOMETIMES WORRY.
THAT MAYBE THE WHOLE DIVORCE THING...
WAS CUZ YOU DIDN'T WANT TO BE WITH ME.
AMELIA! YOU KNOW THAT'S NOT TRUE.
YEAH...WELL... I DON'T KNOW. IT SEEMED THAT WAY SOMETIMES.
I... I DON'T KNOW WHAT TO SAY, AMELIA.
EXCEPT THAT IT'S NOT TRUE.
YOUR MOM AND I AREN'T TOGETHER FOR A LOT OF REASONS, BUT NONE OF THEM ARE YOU.
LOOK... I KNOW THINGS HAVEN'T BEEN THAT GREAT, BUT WE CAN WORK ON THAT.
WHAT DO YOU SAY?
SIGH
YEAH. OKAY.

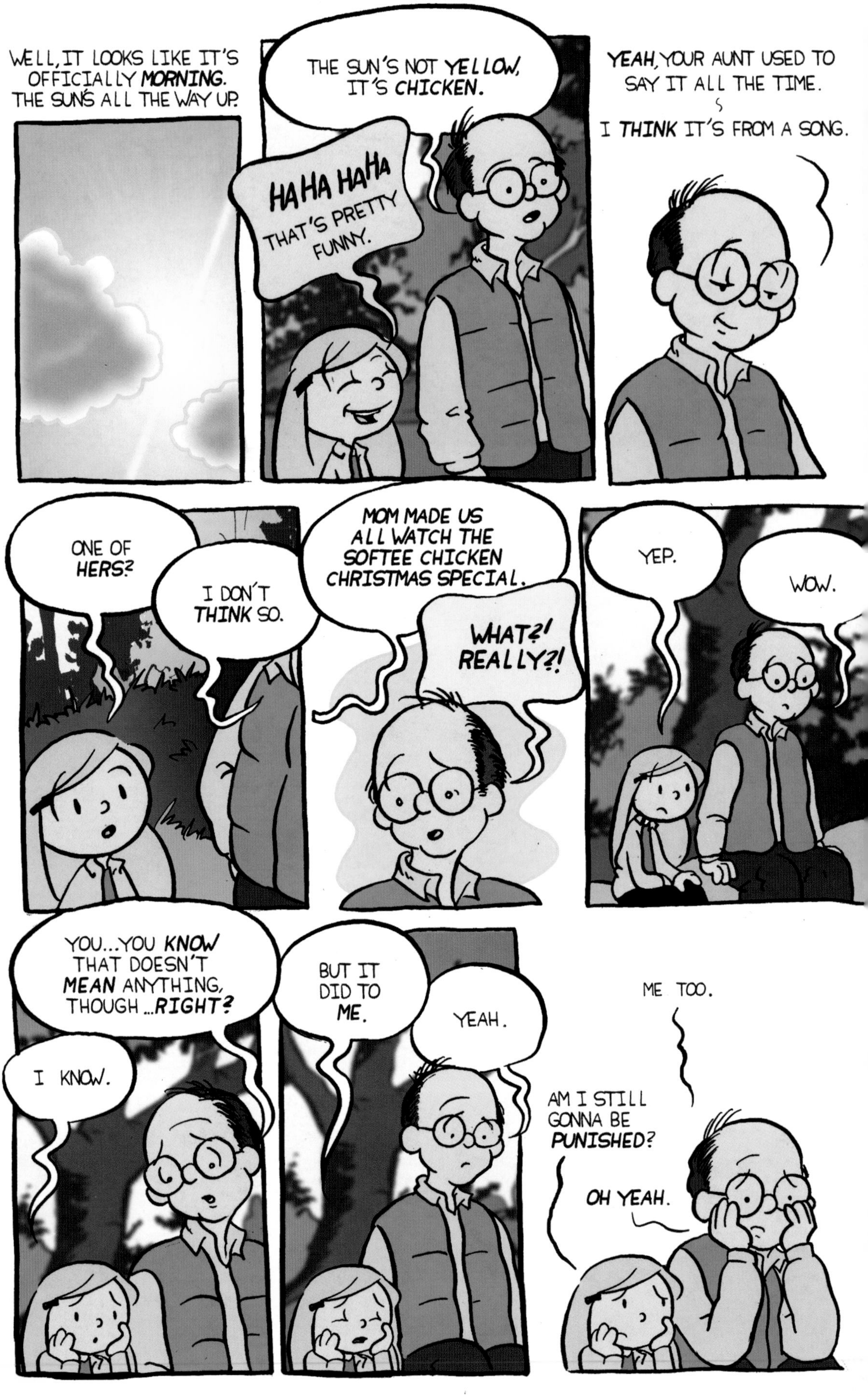
WELL, IT LOOKS LIKE IT'S OFFICIALLY MORNING. THE SUN'S ALL THE WAY UP.
THE SUN'S NOT YELLOW, IT'S CHICKEN.
HAHA HAHA THAT'S PRETTY FUNNY.
YEAH, YOUR AUNT USED TO SAY IT ALL THE TIME.
I THINK IT'S FROM A SONG.
ONE OF HERS?
I DON'T THINK SO.
MOM MADE US ALL WATCH THE SOFTEE CHICKEN CHRISTMAS SPECIAL.
WHAT?! REALLY?!
YEP.
WOW.
YOU...YOU KNOW THAT DOESN'T MEAN ANYTHING, THOUGH ...RIGHT?
I KNOW.
BUT IT DID TO ME.
YEAH.
ME TOO.
AM I STILL GONNA BE PUNISHED?
OH YEAH.

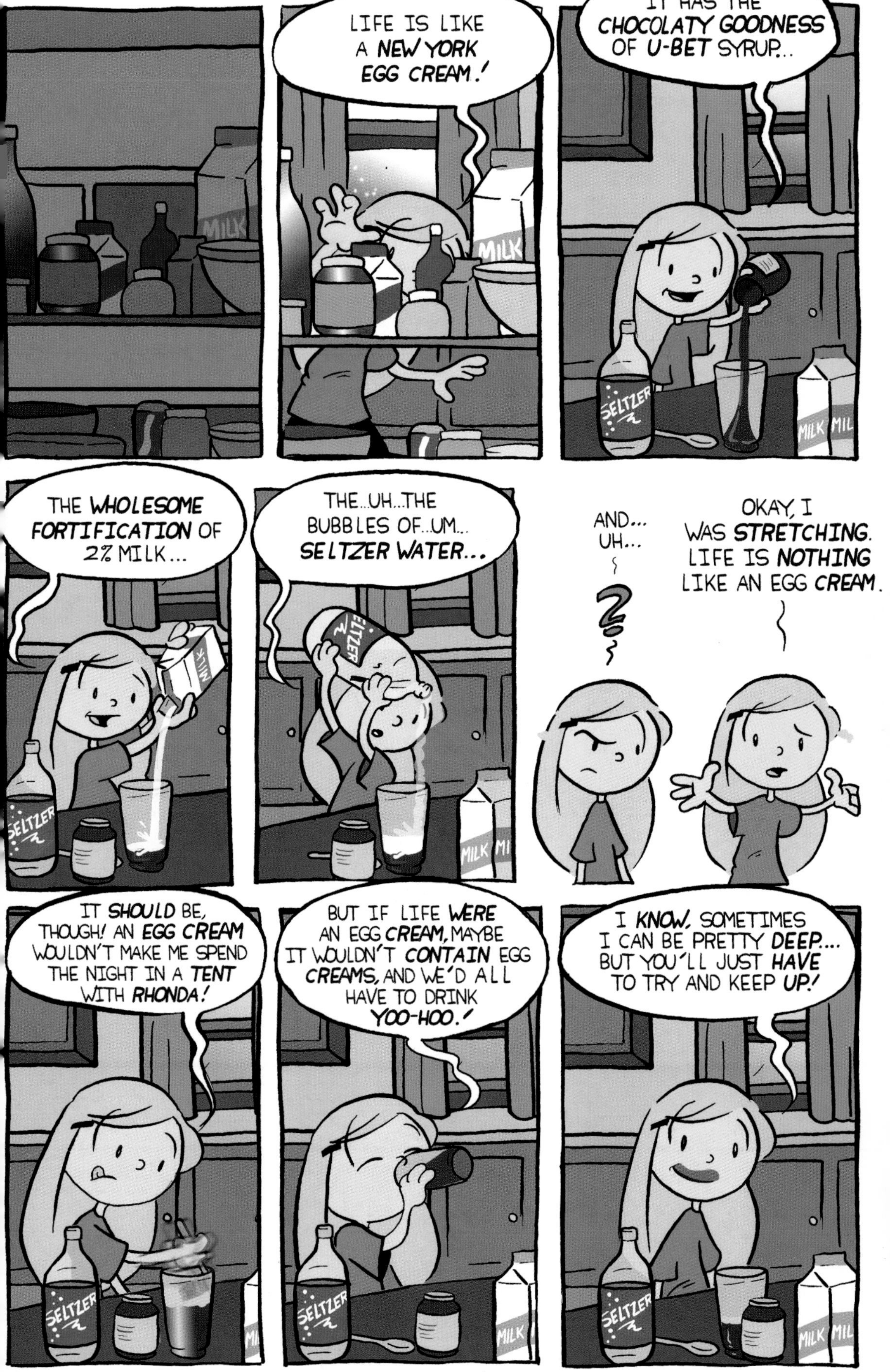
LIFE IS LIKE A NEW YORK EGG CREAM!
IT HAS THE CHOCOLATY GOODNESS OF U-BET SYRUP...
THE WHOLESOME FORTIFICATION OF 2% MILK...
THE...UH...THE BUBBLES OF...UM... SELTZER WATER...
AND... UH...
OKAY, I WAS STRETCHING. LIFE IS NOTHING LIKE AN EGG CREAM.
IT SHOULD BE, THOUGH! AN EGG CREAM WOULDN'T MAKE ME SPEND THE NIGHT IN A TENT WITH RHONDA!
BUT IF LIFE WERE AN EGG CREAM, MAYBE IT WOULDN'T CONTAIN EGG CREAMS, AND WE'D ALL HAVE TO DRINK YOO-HOO!
I KNOW. SOMETIMES I CAN BE PRETTY DEEP... BUT YOU'LL JUST HAVE TO TRY AND KEEP UP!
MILK
SELTZER

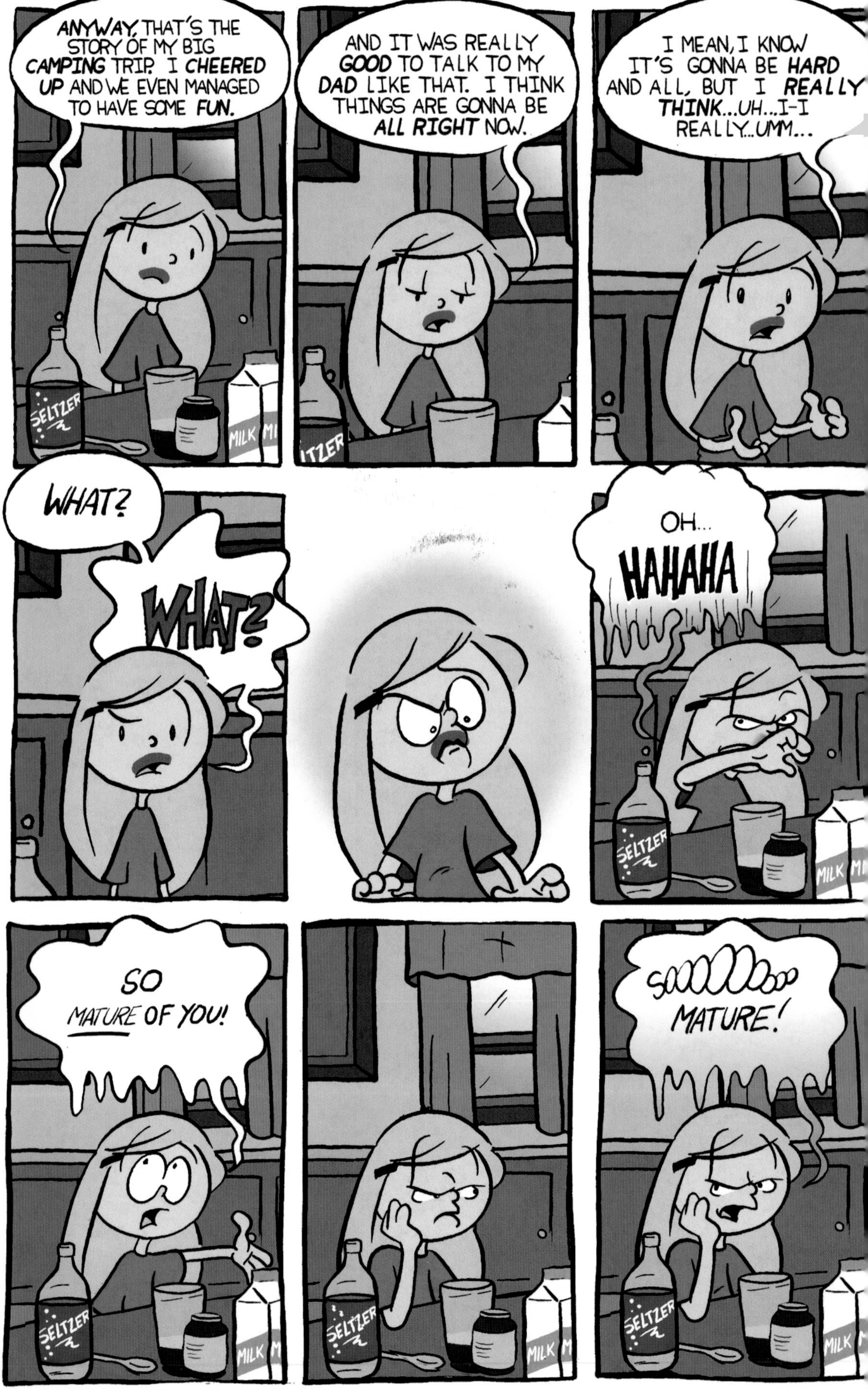
ANYWAY, THAT'S THE STORY OF MY BIG CAMPING TRIP. I CHEERED UP AND WE EVEN MANAGED TO HAVE SOME FUN.
SELTZER
MILK
AND IT WAS REALLY GOOD TO TALK TO MY DAD LIKE THAT. I THINK THINGS ARE GONNA BE ALL RIGHT NOW.
I MEAN, I KNOW IT'S GONNA BE HARD AND ALL, BUT I REALLY THINK...UH...I-I REALLY...UMM...
WHAT?
WHAT?
OH... HAHAHA
SO MATURE OF YOU!
SOOOOOooo MATURE!